STORIES
FROM THE
AFTERLIFE

STORIES FROM THE AFTERLIFE

QUINN DALTON

Press 53
Winston-Salem, North Carolina

Press 53
PO Box 30314
Winston-Salem, NC 27130

First Edition

Cover design by Greg Monroy

Cover photo, "Sunshine of Your Love (Coloured Smoke)" copyright © 2007 by Myla Kent, used by permission of the artist

"Trigger Finger" appeared in *The Southeast Review Online Companion*, fall 2007
"Monks" appeared in *Arkansas Review*, August 2007
"Jimmy the Brain and the Beautiful Aideen" appeared in *Crazyhorse*, summer 2007
"Lowell's Lines" appeared in *Verb*, spring 2007.
"What We Do with Loss" appeared in *Chattahoochee Review*, spring 2007.
"The Music You Never Hear" appeared in *One Story*, August 2005, and again in *New Stories from the South 2006: The Year's Best*.
"Small" appeared in *Gargoyle*, August 2006.
"Plot vs. Character" appeared in *Sex & Sensibility*, an anthology, Simon & Schuster, February 2005.
"Five-Minute Man" appeared in *Indiana Review*, November 2004.
"I Know a Woman" appeared in *American Girls About Town*, an anthology, Simon & Schuster, October 2004.

Printed on acid-free paper

ISBN 978-0-9793049-4-1

for David, Avery and Alia

Contents

Acknowledgments

I would like to thank the editors of the following anthologies and literary journals where these stories originally appeared:

American Girls About Town, Arkansas Review, Chattahoochee Review, Crazyhorse, Gargoyle, Indiana Review, New Stories From The South, One Story, Sex & Sensibility, and *Verb.*

I am lucky to count these fine writers—Julianna Baggott, Julie Funderburk, Mary Ellis Gibson, Andrea Selch, and Lynn York—as my readers and friends.

Thanks to Kevin Watson and Sheryl Monks, publishers of Press 53, for believing in short stories and for seeking mine out. And, as always, I am grateful to Nat Sobel and his excellent staff, especially Emily Russo.

I Know a Woman

L ET'S CALL HER JUDY. I like the simple names that sound as if they could belong to your next door neighbor or the mother of your best friend in second grade. So Judy works for this janitorial company, not doing the jobs, but sales, corporate contracts. This is in a medium-sized town in the southeast, the kind of place where if you live there ten years, as I have, you get to know a lot of people, or at least the connections between them. Anyway, it gets around that Judy strips on the side. This guy she works with named José is telling it; says he gives her half his paycheck every week in tips.

The boss, Dennis, doesn't believe it. Upstanding Christian type— loves God, pays *illegales* cash under the table, that sort of thing. Then one night when Dennis is working late by himself in the office, Judy's twelve-year-old daughter calls, asking for her mother. Dennis says she isn't there. "Must be on her way home," he says, though she left hours ago. The girl says, "I know she's there because she just called me and said she was working late." Dennis says he'll try to find her. He calls Judy's cell phone. No answer. He locks up and gets an idea. He drives past the Dockside Dolls out near the interstate where she's supposedly stripping. He sees her car. He decides he'll call the daughter back and tell her that her mother is working late, and, yes, he'd forgotten that he'd asked her to run some errands or something—he's going to give her some cover, see, because that's a good Christian thing to do, though he's already imagining the solemn confrontation in his office, how he'll tell Judy what he knows, how she'll cry through her confession. But then he realizes he doesn't have her home number with him so he can't call her daughter back.

The next night he drives by again, and again he sees Judy's car. He doesn't have kids himself, doesn't even want them, but he thinks about Judy's daughter, sitting at home alone, waiting for her mother. He wants to go in and drag Judy off the stage. He's enraged, really. And he's scared to go in there. Not because he's never been. He went once on the night before he was married, a bachelor party, of course, and his friends bought him a lap dance, stuffed the money in his pants so the girl had to fish it out. This was before he was saved, understand. She reaches in there and he's hard as a rock and she says, "I love the small ones, honey." So he's nervous. Course he figures that same woman couldn't still be there after four years, and even then she couldn't recognize him in the blur of men that line the stage every night, red-faced, meaty necks rolling over their collars or sweat still glistening on their arms, regulars after their shifts, or, like him, timid men dragged in by their buddies before sacrificing themselves to marriage, giddy with some kind of last meal mentality.

On the third night he pulls into the parking lot at Dockside Dolls and sits there for a while, looking at Judy's car, but can't go in. Another man would've left this alone, wouldn't have even gone to the place. So why Dennis? He wants to *save* her, see. He talks his wife into going with him—he explains he's worried about this employee. The wife decides to bring her sister and her sister's husband because who knows what might happen and they wouldn't want anyone to think that this is what the wife and Dennis do for fun, in secret, when they're not planning pig pickings to pay for new robes for the women's choir. The next night, the four of them walk in the door and find a table. Judy's up there stripping, and pretty soon she's topless, with a little thong panty, shaking her money maker, as they say. She looks good—definitely hasn't had her breasts done like the other girls, who are a little younger and have implants the size of softballs—but she has long legs and slim hips and she knows how to move. Dennis and his wife and her sister and her sister's husband sit there, not sure what to do. Dennis waits for Judy to see them. Eventually she does. She loses the twitch in her hips for a beat. Her face becomes real again—she's looking at them, reacting to them, fighting to regain that blank Barbie doll smile. She dances to the other side of the stage—it's a four-leaf clover, the catwalk a stem, and she stays on the other leaves until the men on their side of the place start complaining, howling and beating the slick stage. Then the music changes and Judy dances back behind the curtain, and another woman comes out.

After that, Dennis and company don't have any reason to stay. There's a two-drink minimum, but Dennis refuses to buy even a ginger ale, and the waitress is getting pissed. So they leave.

Of course, Judy quits pretty much right away. She does it really well. She calls in sick for a week, and Dennis bides his time, thinking she'll eventually come around and confess everything. But what she does instead is tell Dennis she needs to take more sick leave to care for her widowed mother, who's fallen and broken her hip. Doesn't even mention the other night at Dockside Dolls, and Dennis figures he can't bring it up under the circumstances, what with the injured mother in the picture now. Later, after the sick leave checks run out, he learns she's skipped town. No trace. The daughter is left with the grandmother, who, it turns out, is perfectly healthy and, when Dennis calls, is still miffed about a bank account Judy cleaned out. Dennis talks to Judy's landlady, who's been relieved of a microwave, area rug and small freezer that came with the place.

You'd think that would be all. But there's this weird twist: Dennis' wife files for divorce a year to the day after the Dockside Dolls excursion. She puts her half of the janitorial company up for sale, and Dennis is out of a job since he can't buy her out.

Things turn out okay for Judy's daughter, by the way. It's not easy to be abandoned, to be sure, but her grandmother brought her up well, and she's going to start college in the fall—that gives you a sense of where we are now.

And where am I, in this story? I'm the wife. Ex-wife. Usually when I tell about Judy I leave out the more personal details because it only begs the question as to how I know. The way I tell it, I was just working with Judy in the cleaning business at the time, and José, the guy who stuffed half his paycheck in Judy's g-string every week, saw the whole thing.

And I didn't divorce Dennis because of Judy. Not specifically. See, there are some details you'd have to smooth over if you decided to tell this story while sitting, say, at a ten-top in the City Club for a Dinner for Qualified Investors, "...with investable assets of $1,000,000 or more," to discuss Comprehensive Wealth Management. Let me note here that I have nowhere near a million dollars, even if I sold everything I owned, which isn't much. I think I look the part in my sage green silk suit cut loose like a man's, but the fabric unmistakably female. I like that about it—the form being one thing and the details being something else.

Anyway, in this dining scenario, should I find myself telling this story, Judy would be an employee of mine in a business I once owned and have since sold, not that far from the truth, and it would be a story about the secret, desperate lives of the middle class. Something to get the table warmed up. It would be that rather than the story of a woman married a few years out of college to an older man who'd found God while building his business on the backs of migrant farm workers. But yes, it would still be a story of escape.

I am from a small town where people dropped out of high school in their rush to gain employment in the mills. I hadn't done anything in life except sell cleaning contracts with Judy. Dennis explained to me we'd never have time for kids; we worked too much. When we went to Dockside Dolls to see Judy that night, I knew I'd never forget it.

At the City Club, I'm sitting next to John, who owns Poseidon, a national business-to-business supplier of tropical fish, tanks, pumps, and maintenance services. He hands me his card, which is, predictably, light blue with a sparkling angelfish on the left side, next to his name. John tells me that exotic fish are the rage. "Doctor's offices buy them to keep the patients in the waiting room calm. Bigwigs buy them for the executive offices. Night clubs and hotels love 'em. There's one of mine over there." Flat blue eyes, shiny skin, soft white fingers sweeping to direct my attention to the far wall next to the hostess stand. A small shark swims sluggishly in the purple lit water. He seems perfectly at home in his circumstances, or maybe just resigned.

The seat to my left is empty. Next to John sits Karen, CEO of the Center for Business and Behavioral Research, where executives go to spend three days to two weeks flinging themselves backwards off of platforms into each other's arms and taking seminars on how to treat their employees like human beings or appear as if they are doing so. Karen comes over with her card. She is blond, neatly wedged into an ivory sheath dress with gold buttons, a knuckle-sized knot of gold in each earlobe. She's about to ask me what my deal is when a man slips quietly into the seat on my left. I don't even notice him until I feel the wool of his suit sleeve brush my arm. He introduces himself as Neil. It just so happens that Neil works for the brokerage firm that is sponsoring this dinner for High Net Worth clients, as the invitation noted. Neil hands me his card. "And you are?" he asks, with deep and gentle interest, like a doctor inquiring as to how much pain I am in.

I had chosen the table in the back, the seat nearest the door. I have no idea how I got on the mailing list, but I thought this would be fun. I have a little money, sure, from the sale of my half of the business. I have a condo in one of those older buildings where you pay for the architectural details and you get used to your neighbors pacing over the floorboards, phones ringing quietly up and down the hall, muffled as if under water.

I offer my hand to Neil and he shakes it softly. Almost just holding it, really. "Neil," I tell him, "I need to make a quick phone call."

I step out of the room, flipping open my cell. I decide to call my sister. Usually I tell her when I'm doing something like this—going to a support group for a condition I don't have, slipping into pink, hushed funeral parlors and saying goodbye to people I never knew, or hobnobbing with this town's eager elite. She doesn't necessarily discourage me. She married an older man, too. He is away often on business, just like our father was before he retired, a traveling salesman. So maybe we both married our father. Except her husband Ed is a lot nicer than Dennis or our father ever were.

Sasha picks up on the first ring. "What are you doing?" I say.

"Reading an article about this guy who married a woman his friends picked out for him in the Mall of America."

"They picked her out in the Mall of America? Do they sell women there?"

"No, they got married there. His friends took applications from women and chose the bride."

It's six o'clock, and I figure she's just gotten home from work. "Sasha, I'm at the City Club at a millionaires dinner."

"Really?" I hear the catch in her voice; she's sitting forward in her chair.

"Seriously. You have to have a million in investable assets to come."

"A million?"

"Investable. Cash." Everyone agrees that I take after my father and my sister takes after our mother, who is athletic, efficient and shy. Like my father, I can sell almost anyone on anything, and I can make friends with anybody, even the dying, the grieving and the rich. "What do you think I should be?" I ask.

Sasha's thinking. I can hear her breathing into the phone. We've done this dozens of times. She gives me a story, and I make people believe it. When I told her I wanted to divorce Dennis and make it cost him, she helped me think up hiring an auditor to value the company—the story was to see how we could save in taxes. I got all the numbers I needed right under his nose. "How about a matchmaker?" she says.

"A matchmaker."

"Yeah, one of those really expensive ones. I saw a full-page ad in a magazine one time. This woman with bleached hair and a pink suit talking about her discrete services, success rates."

"Sasha, that's not the same thing," I say. Sasha's one of those satisfied people, so sometimes she misses details. She's happy with her office job and her working man and a house with little window boxes. She likes going out to eat and renting movies. I might be all the excitement she needs. "Were you looking at some kind of skin magazine?" I ask her, and I think of Judy, I can't help it. I wonder what she did after she disappeared. I keep expecting her to turn up in a new generation of the forbidden—Internet babe, reality TV show queen—but maybe she got rich! Maybe she founded a colony on some lush island. I want to know what she did next, so then maybe I'll know what to do.

In the dining room someone's tapping the microphone, and there's the shuffling of slick-bottomed shoes on low-pile carpet as people turn their attention to the podium. I could leave now, but I know I won't. It's too attractive, this sea of dark suits and bright dresses flitting across the room as people find their seats. The walls are practically all glass up here, and through the open door I can see the late-spring sky shifting to a liquid purple, and the light seems thick enough to float in.

Sasha laughs. She loves me. I don't deserve so much love. "Listen," she says. "She's a matchmaker, not the other. She charges ten thousand a pop!"

"OK. Ten thousand a pop. I'm on it."

Back in the dining room, no one's taken my seat, probably because Neil has draped my swan-folded napkin, which I hadn't even moved from my plate, over the back of my chair. When Neil sees me, he stands and pulls my chair back from the table with his right hand and lifts my napkin. As he turns to face me, I see that he has no left hand. At first I think his suit jacket is too long on that side, but another glance makes it clear.

Now there, I think, is a story.

When I look up to meet his eyes, Neil smiles at me, professional, yet intimate, as if we've been doing business for years. He's tall and good-looking, but not in an aggressive sort of way, really. He has lovely brown eyes. I can't tell what his smile means, though. Is he waiting for me to ask about his hand so we can get it over with? Is he on the lookout for imposters?

I sit and he moves my chair smoothly to the table, then settles himself beside me. "Cocktail?" he asks me.

"Sure," I say. "How nice of you to save my seat."

Everyone around me is ordering scotch rocks or martinis with a twist, so I order a margarita. "Tell me," I ask the waiter. "Are your margaritas pre-mixed?"

He nods regretfully. He's a college kid and nervous, maybe he's new on the job. I'm nervous, too, but it's a good kind of nervous, different from the kind that hit me when I realized my husband had acquired me like cleaning equipment, that he expected to get his use out of me. *Depreciation* is the word that came to mind. "I want a top shelf, then," I say.

The kid looks at me blankly.

"One shot of Cuervo, one of Grand Marnier, and one of lime juice, shaken on rocks, salt," I tell him. He stands there writing for a while, and I wait until he looks up. "You're a sweetie," I say, and he smiles, and I love to see a young man smile.

This little comment makes Neil's head snap up from the pad he's been making notes on during my exchange with the waiter. He cradles the pad in his left arm. I have no idea what he could be writing; the first speaker is just now introducing himself. Then Neil nudges the pad in my direction. GUEST LIST, he's written at the top. And, on the next line: NAME, COMPANY, PHONE/E-MAIL.

I know then that Neil's on to me. He already has everyone's business cards, a neat stack by his dessert plate. It's a thrill. I've never been caught before. I take his pen, still warm from his hand, and make up a name. I write "Matchmaker" under COMPANY. Under PHONE/E-MAIL I add: "I notice you don't wear a wedding ring, Neil. Would you be interested in a consultation? Discrete, only the best people."

I realize this is a little cruel. In any case, it's possible he's married, but of course there's no way to tell. I tear the paper off the pad. Everyone at the table glances at me, and I smile, and just then the drinks come, which distracts them as I fold the paper twice and hand it back to Neil with his pad and heavy fountain pen.

Neil lays the paper on his plate, anchors it with his arm, unfolds it slowly. He reads it, leans over to me, whispers in my ear. "I think you should go."

I NEVER REALLY QUIT DRINKING after Dennis got saved. I just had these notions about growing with the marriage and being sensitive to one's partner's needs, etcetera, and so I tried my best. I'd sneak a drink at Sasha's house when I could. A sip of wine became almost erotic, the warmth spreading on the tongue. I carried a toothbrush everywhere.

How it started—Dennis told me one day that he'd dreamed of a wall of water standing over our house, and that the wall of water had spoken to him. It had said, "Go forth."

"Go forth?" I remember asking. I said, "Have you been watching Charlton Heston movies? Moses and so on?"

Dennis looked at me the way I imagine a wall of water would look at you if it had narrowed eyes and rather bushy brown hair dusted with gray. He towered. He quivered with anger about to spill over. "I'm telling you about God speaking to me and you ask me about movies?"

I decided to try. I decided that once the waters had parted, and the new path was revealed, it was better to take your chances. Dennis told me the dream meant service. He picked out a church, and we started going to hear people play rock and roll hymns with guitars and synthesizers and waving arms. They didn't drink, so Dennis stopped, and I pretended. He joined the choir and started nailing houses together on weekends. It was noble work, but walking around with a hammer in my hand and no clue of what to do with it made me feel heavy and exhausted. I hadn't gone to church as a child. I wasn't prepared for the fellowship, the hugging. I only made one friend in that whole church, a woman who later died, but not before she told me that there was, in fact, no path.

I SIT AT THE LOBBY BAR for a while. I haven't eaten anything but ancient peanuts and cheese crackers from the snack bowl since getting kicked out of the City Club (and, thinking fast, taking the margarita with me). It's too depressing to call Sasha; I'm putting it off, not answering when she calls me. At about eight Neil steps through the brushed steel elevator doors with a pack of men in dark suits. He's the youngest one in the group. He carries the projector screen, a satchel strapped diagonally across his chest. His hair is nearly black, cut close, and as he looks up at the ceiling, laughing at something, I can see the pale cords of his neck. I decide to focus my energy on him as if I had just spoken to him. I decide that's as close as I'll ever get to praying.

He looks at me. I don't raise my eyebrows or wiggle a little greeting with my fingers. I look back at him, and wait to see if he walks over.

He does. He's very smooth about it, waving off his suit friends with his handless arm; maybe he's telling them he's forgotten something upstairs and he'll see them in the morning.

Neil takes his time getting over to me, threading the projection screen through the cluster of low tables. He sets the screen down, slides his bag off of his shoulder and stands in front of me with his good hand—his *present* hand—in his pocket. His other arm hangs relaxed at his side. "So, did you sign anyone up tonight?" I ask him. "Get some juicy commissions?"

He leans against the bar and looks at me. He smiles, not the professional, solicitous smile from the City Club, but still friendly, amused. I amuse him. That's fine with me. Generally, I don't amuse anyone except Sasha. "You know, it's usually men who try to sneak into these things," he says.

"Why so top secret?" I ask, swiveling on the stool. "What are you really doing up there, anyway?"

Neil signals the bartender by lifting one finger, points to the tap for a beer. His hand is quite graceful. "You didn't miss anything," he says. "I got cornered by the fish guy who started raving about cichlids. Did you know a school can clean the meat off a human in less than a minute? And Karen invited me to try out their sensory deprivation tank." Neil flips the napkin the bartender set out with his drink. "The last guy who snuck in was a Vespa salesman. You know those little scooters that sound like a distressed mouse?"

"I wonder why it's always men," I muse. I also wonder why Neil is talking to me at all. I'm making myself a little dizzy, swiveling back and forth on the stool, but it's probably also hunger, and my curiosity.

"That is a good question," Neil says, sipping his draft. "This guy just wanted some customers, I think."

"That's all I wanted."

Neil looks at me, one eyebrow raised.

I chomp down on a disintegrating peanut. "I'm a matchmaker, remember?"

"Give me a break," Neil says. And then leans forward as if he's about to kiss me, but he doesn't. His eyes are inches from mine. "What do you really do?" he asks me, staying close.

I'm not sure if he's asking about my work, but I answer that way. "I have some investments," I say. "Nothing specific, really. A little consulting here and there." That's all I feel I need to tell him, or anyone. I think we're rather obsessed with this career stuff. Who cares, if I'm paying the bills? I touch Neil's arm, the one closest to me, the one that ends too soon. "Listen," I say. "I know this woman."

I don't tell him about Judy. I tell him the other important story, about this woman from Caribou, Maine who joined a church down here with a huge singles Bible study group. Who knows what made her migrate all this way? Well, she proceeds to sleep with all the men in the singles group. Nobody tells, it's too good a thing; they don't want the women to find out.

The women love her. They've adopted her because when she came to town she was living out of her van. She becomes their project. They find her an apartment, they perm her hair, they take her shopping and teach her beauty tips they've collected over the years, like dabbing a touch of frosted gloss in the center of the lip over matte lipstick to make the mouth look fuller, or swiping pale shadow in the inner corners of the eyes to make them look farther apart. It all helps her campaign with the men in the group. She gets an office job and goes to every church function. She doesn't drink, she always looks great. When she wants to go to bed with a man, she comes up to him during social hour with, say, a cup of Kool-Aid in her hand, her lips shiny and red with it, and she talks to him for a few minutes. Then she waits until she's sure no one is looking and touches him in a way that makes him know he's chosen—brushes his hip or squeezes his wrist, and asks him to come over to her brand new apartment later.

After a while, she runs through the singles group and moves on to the men's choir, starts with the tenors. Takes up with a married guy. The tenor falls in love with her. He gets a night with her and he's hooked. He begins calling her all the time, he buys her things, but she isn't interested. She moves on to other men. He threatens her one night and she leaves town all in a hurry in her van. Apparently, she's been threatened before and does not think it's a joke. He hears she's gone back up to Caribou. He hires a private investigator up there. The PI tracks her down; he's parked on a street in Caribou one morning, watching her walk to work. PI's somehow gotten her cell phone number. He calls the tenor from his own cell, gives him the number. The tenor calls. The woman answers, hears his voice, drops her phone and runs away. The detective says, "She moved to another state, man, to get away from you. You need to leave her alone."

When I finish telling this to Neil, he takes it in for a little while, tapping his glass with his one thumb. He says, "I don't even think you've told me your real name." He smiles at me as if he's just bet me on whether I can stand on my head. He isn't going to ask any questions about this story of mine.

I say, "That guy with the detective, that was my husband."

Neil, still gazing at his beer, does not move a muscle. I can see he must be good at what he does, advising millionaires.

I say, "I want you to know, I don't hold a grudge."

There's another, related part of the story that for now I'll leave out: That night when Dennis took me and Sasha and Ed with him to see Judy, that was the beginning of my new life. Some people go to church or AA to start over; I did it at a strip club. I didn't know it at the time, or if I did, I couldn't admit it to myself right then. When Dennis told me he wanted to save Judy, my mind rattled back and forth between imagining him striding across the stage and striking her on the forehead with the heel of his hand like a revival preacher and me climbing on the stage to dance, just for him, in a way that would save us both.

I'd invited Sasha and Ed to come with us so I could sneak sips from their drinks. I figured a little alcohol might be nice—it didn't take much for me to get a buzz. I actually wondered if I'd enjoy myself. But the fact was, the place was depressing. I guess I wasn't prepared for the number of overfed men in gray suits, road warriors who looked not all that different from my father at the end of one of his trips—that traveler's stare, disoriented and bored. Or the businesslike way Judy and the other woman worked the stage. Except for that one moment when she saw us and we saw her. She looked straight at me. We went on sales calls together every day, but right then she could have been anyone. Her nakedness was like a cloak. She looked at Dennis, and he leaned forward in his chair, as if ready to pounce. Then she looked at me and turned hard on her spike heels, and I knew I wouldn't see her again; she would get away clean.

Neil pulls up a stool next to me. He leans to tuck his projector screen against the foot of the bar, to keep it out of the way so no one trips over it. He's a thoughtful man. He says, "I went to high school with a girl who had been missing for fifteen years. Her babysitter stole her. She walked into a sheriff's office outside of Phoenix and turned herself in. They found her mother in Milwaukee—ex-drug addict, never reported it. The girl, Cass, was seventeen and they gave her a test and put her in tenth grade." He folds his fingers around his beer. "We had a class together. Algebra. I failed it."

"So you failed algebra and you're from Milwaukee?" I ask.

"Yes, that was exactly my point," Neil says. He taps one finger against his lips, smiling at me. He pushes his glass toward the bartender for another draft. "Actually," he says, "She was the only one who would date me after my brother cut off my hand."

Obviously, the version I'm getting of this story is intended to jolt. It works. I look at him with my eyebrows raised, waiting.

"Of course, it was an accident," Neil says. He's in no hurry; it's his turn now. "We were hiking Lake Peak outside of Santa Fe. It was early in the season, chilly, but no big deal. There's some amazing views..." his voice trails off. He sits with both elbows on the bar now, a secret up his sleeve. "There's some drop offs, and we decided to climb down one a ways, then back up, for fun. Well, I went first, stumbled, started a small avalanche. I remember thinking I would get through it. I don't believe what people say about their lives flashing. All I saw was the rocks falling. Then I was on my back, my shoulder up against the mountain, my hand under a rock. On my other side, I could see the rest of the way down. My brother climbed down, tried to get me free. He couldn't get leverage in such a tight spot, and there was the danger of making more rocks fall if he moved that one. I don't remember much. I was bleeding a lot. We spent the night there together, no cell phones back then. Nobody on the trail; it was too cold. My brother tied off my arm with his sweatshirt. In the morning, he cut me free. We talked about it for a while, whether we should do it, but it was hard, because I kept blacking out. The cutting woke me up, though. He hauled me back up. I held onto his neck. Good thing it happened to me instead of him. He's the bigger one. We both would have died, maybe."

"He saved you," I whisper, but Neil hears me.

"He wrote me a letter about it while I was in the hospital. He wanted me to know about every moment. He wanted to know if he should go back and get my hand."

"What did you say?" I ask. My stomach is solid in my belly.

"He felt guilty, you know," Neil says. He doesn't flinch when I put my hand on his arm. I can feel where the warmth ends. He says, "I told him I had everything I needed, and that he shouldn't worry."

You can never predict the cost of escape. Not too long after Judy disappeared, the woman from Caribou, Maine, whose name is too pretty to mention, showed my husband what she thought of a good tenor. She was already in town the night we paid our visit to Judy. She was probably getting her eyebrows plucked and her hair highlighted by the huggy, well-meaning women in our church. Maybe Dennis would have fallen for her anyway, naked Judy or not. Maybe everything was going along just as his God intended. But I like to think that the night at Dockside Dolls was pivotal. I like to think my story has shape.

"It wasn't all bad for me at Dennis' church." I say. "There was this woman I really liked. Her name was Amelia. She was older, with really short white hair and gray eyes that changed color depending on what she wore. One day she started to notice little metallic flakes in her fingernails. At first, just one or two, but then they became streaks of silver. She went to her doctor, her herbalist; no one knew what to do. So she decided not to worry about it.

25

Then I found out about Dennis and the woman from Caribou. My sister was coaching me on pitching the business audit to Dennis so I could get my cut once I divorced him, but mostly I just wanted to disappear. I went to Amelia. I guess I was hoping for a sign. When I asked her if there was some way I could understand what path God wanted me to take, she shook her head. She said, 'You're asking for something that doesn't exist'."

I stop to catch my breath; I've been talking fast. Neil opens his mouth to interrupt me but I keep going. "By then," I continue, "Her nails were almost completely silver—I mean, you could see the skin beneath the nails, but the silver was cloudy; it looked like metal shining up from the bottom of a lake."

Neil says, "And so that was it? She said she didn't have an answer for you and you took it?" He shakes his head. "I don't believe you, whoever you are." He pulls his arm away from me but I reach for it again.

"Don't give up on me yet," I say. "You're right, I begged her. I cried and told her I couldn't take the hard answers right then; I needed something specific. She said whatever I needed, I had it in me. Something like that; anyway, it wasn't what I wanted to hear," I tell him. But that isn't really all: after she told me what I had in me, she showed me the backs of her hands, fingers spread wide, nails flashing, as if to offer evidence.

"Hers was the first funeral I ever crashed," I say. "Her family didn't like the church since she'd willed everything to it instead of them, and I guess I can't blame them. So it was a family-only affair, small. I slipped right in there, though."

"And were you happy you did?" Neil turns his arm under my hand, so that the part where it ends, right above the wrist, is facing up. He lets me slide my hand inside his shirtsleeve and I can feel where the flesh has scarred over the bone, protecting it. I think we could both be naked, and I wouldn't be anymore scared than I am now. I think of that night when I saw Judy's pale breasts colored pink and purple in the circling lights, how she revealed us.

"At the time, no, I wasn't happy about it," I say. Neil is sitting very still, my fingers on him, reading him. "I was sad. I was there because I loved her. The family had requested a closed casket, you know," I say. This was for me the saddest part. I had walked in there expecting to see those beautiful hands crossed over her chest. I wanted to see them one more time, because—and I'm going to try to explain this as accurately as I can—when she had showed me her nails the last time I visited her, the fingers fanned out like that, I saw how the future comes out of you, mysterious and shining, and there's nothing for you to do except move into it, naked and willing to leave everything you once knew.

The Music You Never Hear

DOBI CAME TO HELP when Martha started dying. Martha had been sick before, and he was used to what that looked like, her eyes over-focused with pain and then medicine-blank. Then, her needs were simple—broth, painkillers, the TV kept low. His daughters took care of most of it. They were grown and married with children of their own, but they took turns sitting with her until Dobi came for the night, because he was still on the road then, home only on weekends, his suitcase smelling of hot pavement and hotel rooms.

Dobi was nineteen. She wasn't a nurse really, just a housekeeper who was willing to sleep at white people's houses. You couldn't find many white women willing to stay overnight, and the ones who would took to stealing the drugs, a pill or two at a time. He came home from one trip to find Martha sleeping on shit-smeared sheets. Dobi had never let anything like that happen. She kept the house smelling of Pine Sol and spray starch. She had even graduated from high school, not typical. Later she told him, when he asked if she'd ever thought of leaving, that she'd wanted to go to nursing school, but the nearest one was two states away, and she was the youngest and the only daughter, her brothers off married or working, and so it was understood she would be the one to care for her parents.

In 1953, the town was hardly a town, but a cross formed by the river and the railroad tracks. Above the tracks were the few commercial streets and the Highlands neighborhood, where he and Martha had grown up and established their own household, where their daughters lived, now, too. South of the river were the mills and the docks; you could hear the hollow horns from Dobi's house, even with all the windows shut tight, he learned later.

Martha had taught French for twenty-six years and played the piano so well she could reproduce anything she heard without sheet music. She had few faults—a tendency to lose household items like bottle openers or garden gloves or even the occasional bill, and a habit of snacking in the middle of the night when she woke up to go to the bathroom, so she was always plump in the earlier years, though she ate hardly anything at meals. But he had enjoyed these things about her; they made her human, because in every other way she was so gentle and cultured and even-tempered, he had always felt a little beneath her. Not in such a way as to make him want to demean her, the way he'd seen other men put down their wives to remind them who was boss. He was simply mindful that she had come from a better family and in general had better manners and intellect than he. And she was tough—she had held off the disease more than once. But by the time Dobi started tending her, she had gotten tired, as anybody would, the skin of her face and arms slack, her chest a gray drape, her hair and nails yellowed from medication.

YEARS LATER, when the boy was old enough, Ned took him to other towns to see minor league baseball games in the summer. Nobody knew them there, and while Alfred was small nobody held them to the colored seating rules. Occasionally, some drunk would ask *That your shoe-shine boy?* Ned pretended not to hear it, and Alfred, brown eyes shining up at him, did the same. The boy was a watcher, this was indisputable.

The outings continued until Alfred turned eight, and Dobi finally married. Until then, Ned had sent cash so it wouldn't show in his account. Mailing it meant he didn't have to hand it to her on his visits, and it wouldn't need to be acknowledged. It never was.

DOBI'S HOUSE WAS A FOUR-ROOM SHOTGUN on the edge of the Johnson's four hundred acres that Dobi's father and, later, her brothers, sharecropped. Dobi's parents had the bedroom; Dobi and Alfred slept on a cot in the front room, or on the porch, depending on the weather. Ned had no idea how it had worked when her four brothers had still lived there; there weren't even that many chairs around the kitchen table.

When Ned brought ice cream on one of his first visits, they had to eat it right then because there was no freezer. Dobi served it in chipped, rose-patterned bowls. The gold on the rims had mostly flaked away. Dobi's parents ate shyly, smiling almost apologetically as they sipped the melting cream from their spoons. Dobi would not even look at him, but he could still enjoy the boy, happily stretching his mouth for each giant spoonful of vanilla. Dobi ate some, too, but with no expression on her face. Not rude or ungrateful, but as if she were eating alone and had no idea she was being watched.

He didn't think he was saving his soul, doing this. He just couldn't imagine how one could do it differently, in this world, where there were certain places one could sit or not sit, and yet there was also this pleasure in watching the boy's milk-coated pink mouth, his eyes closing and then opening wide with joy. He could take pleasure in this, in the coldness of his own tongue on a hot day, in seeing Dobi receive something from him, regardless of whether she'd wanted it.

SHE HAD BEEN OUT OF HIGH SCHOOL a year when she started caring for Martha. She fed and bathed her, emptied bed pans. One time, Dobi found him standing with the laundry bucket open, staring at the soiled, clotted diapers. He'd caught an overnight train and hadn't slept. He'd entered the house quietly, knowing from the white flash of sheets on the backyard line that Dobi was there. His daughters left the washing to her. He told himself he was slipping in to make sure Dobi was acting right even when unsupervised, but in truth he had done it to avoid being confronted immediately with the bustling energy of someone who had come there to work. Martha had become someone's job, but, standing silently in the kitchen, he'd wanted to pretend for a moment that this wasn't the case, that she was only napping, and soon she would get up and finish potting plants and make him dinner.

Then he noticed the laundry bucket sitting at the end of the hall; Dobi had probably carried it from the bedroom and was planning to take it to the basement to wash. He heard her quietly talking to Martha. He could not discern the words, just the soothing, comforting tone of her voice—it could have been Martha, rocking one of their daughters to sleep. Overcome with this memory, he leaned without thinking to open the laundry bucket. The force of the smell dizzied him. Just then, Dobi stepped into the hall. Without a word, she met him where he stood, picked up the bucket and carried it away, and he never saw it again.

HE GOT USED TO SEEING HER, yet sometimes he was struck by her foreignness in his house. The house over time had become an extension of Martha—the pastel walls, the softly curved couches, the powder-gray carpeting, the quiet interrupted in their later years only by her piano playing, while she could still do it, and by the evening news. In contrast, Dobi moved like a pencil line through the rooms, dark and precise. Her short waist emphasized her long arms and legs and her small, high breasts. The skin on the backs of her arms and her collarbones shone, as if she'd rubbed them with oil.

She lived there more than he did for two years; that was the truth. When he was on the road, he was a heartily laughing salesman of industrial tubing. He'd come home, sometimes after traveling all night, weak and silent with exhaustion—he couldn't do it much longer, he knew; it wasn't the adventure it had once been—and Dobi would fix him a meal and tell him things about Martha. Good things. "She sat up for two hours," Dobi would say. Or, "She fed herself half a cup of pudding." As if Martha was a friend accompanied to a movie, or shopping—not a dying woman whose pension paid for as much comfort as could be delivered. Dobi meant to be encouraging, he knew, but Martha's small victories were only a signal of smaller ones to come, until there were none.

THE DOCTOR PRESCRIBED MORPHINE during the final weeks. He came and taught Dobi how to tie off the arm with a strip of rubber, slide in the needle. When Dobi left the room for a moment, the doctor turned to Ned. The pink skin around his eyes was puffed with fat. "We can send out a nurse," he said.

Ned looked at Martha, her eyes closed as if sealed now, her arm stretched over the folded lip of the sheets, palm up, as if testing the air for rain. "She's been with us two years," he said. "Martha's used to her." Strange, he thought, to talk about what Martha was used to—she hadn't spoken a word in over a year at that point.

ONE MORNING WHEN HE CAME HOME from traveling all night, Dobi made eggs and sausage and toast. It was after Dobi had started staying six nights a week, even if one of his daughters could be there too, but before the morphine started—this was how he'd begun to measure time. She said something about Martha's medication, how she'd started giving two smaller doses rather than one large one and now Martha seemed more comfortable. He said, "You should study to be a nurse. You're smart enough, surely." He'd meant it as a compliment, but Dobi's calm face didn't seem to register any pleasure at his recognition of her intellect.

He wanted to say that he respected learning; after all, he'd offered to send both his daughters to college, and few girls from their town had had such an opportunity. "Well, their mother, being a teacher, insisted they go past high school even though we didn't have the money back then," he said. Nelda, the older one, had gotten her teacher's certificate, though she hadn't used it, getting married soon after college to a salesman. She joked that she'd repeated her parents' lives, while Elizabeth had married right out of high school to an electrician. That had been the only time he remembered his daughters not getting along, because Elizabeth had wanted her best friend to be her maid of honor instead of Nelda. Maybe also because Elizabeth was younger and married first. He didn't know; it had blown over, and Nelda had been her maid of honor after all.

Dobi turned cold water on the hissing frying pan. "They's a school for nursing, but it's too far." She began scrubbing and said nothing else. So he asked how she got the name Dobi.

"That's not my given name, it's just short for Deborah," she said.

"Your mother's pet name for you?"

"What her boss lady called me. But it stuck," she said.

He rose from the table. He felt that whatever he said was wounding her, but he wasn't sure; he was just so tired, and dreading walking in to see Martha, and hating himself for dreading it. "How is she?" he asked, feeling foolish, as if there could be any change for the better.

"She's asleep," Dobi said.

"I bought you something," he said, suddenly, though he had not bought her anything at all. She didn't exist for him when he wasn't home, he realized. And when he thought of Martha, he didn't see her gray-faced in her bed, which had been their bed, but twenty, thirty years younger, dressing for church, leaning forward, settling her breasts into a brassiere.

Dobi took his plate. "You don't need to buy me anything, now."

"But I did. I bought it the last trip and forgot about it." He was surprised at how casually the lie came to him. "It's still in my suitcase." He picked it up from the foyer where he'd left it and carried it down the hall to his room, which had been the girls' room. He slept in the twin bed closest to the door, under a flowered spread, when he was there. Dobi napped in the guest room, he supposed, though he had never actually seen her asleep.

He put his suitcase on the twin bed next to the wall, opened it, and walked quietly across the hall to Martha's room. He hoped Dobi hadn't heard him, as she was still cleaning the kitchen. He slowly closed the door behind him, leaving it cracked as it had been when he'd come in, and waited for his eyes to adjust to the dark. The brocade curtains were drawn, but a seam of light showed along one side. Martha was propped on several pillows, her knees propped, too, under the blanket. The bedside table was lined with white cloths, on which rested brown glass bottles, a case of syringes, a special drinking glass with a top so it wouldn't spill.

He could barely discern the rise and fall of Martha's chest. The bridge of her nose was the only smooth part of her face, the skin white as bone. He leaned down to kiss it, and breathed in her medicine and talcum-powdered scent. Then he turned to the wardrobe, which had been her mother's, and drew from the bottom shelf the hand-painted jewelry box he'd bought her in Germany before the war.

He found the necklace in the purple velvet box with white satin lining in which he'd first presented it to her, a few months before they'd become engaged. It was a hair-thin gold chain with a single pearl framed by two gold beads. He'd given it to her for Christmas, and her delight had signaled he should take the next step. He'd always been a cautious man, a man who watched for cues from other people, and he believed this was what had made him successful in sales. He wasn't prematurely aggressive. People appreciated that.

He didn't realize he'd been looking for that necklace until he'd seen the box. The chain rested light and cool as a line of water on his knuckles. It would look completely different on Dobi. Instead of receding so that only the faint outline of pearl shone at the hollow of the throat, as it had on Martha, it would glitter against Dobi's skin, the way her teeth seemed to glow behind her brown lips. He worried then what might happen if one of his daughters saw her wearing it, but he decided he would just tell them in advance of his decision to give a gift from the family. They might be angry but they couldn't defy him.

Martha had told him once that she wanted to be buried in that necklace and with her simple gold wedding band. "You should pass the engagement ring on," she said, not specifying to which daughter, "or sell it. Or keep it. But the necklace was the promise, when we decided. Wasn't it?" she'd asked, and he'd nodded, of course, though he didn't clearly remember knowing he would marry her until after he'd given it to her.

Then she'd said something unexpected. They'd been married thirty years at that point. They were in their early fifties; she'd beaten back the first wave of the disease. He hadn't wanted to see her sick or in pain, but he did feel a last remaining veil had been peeled away, and in some way he knew her better, and he was grateful to have known her, even in her worst moments.

She said, "I don't know if there is a God. Maybe I'll just rot in the ground."

He looked at her, and perhaps she could read the alarm in his eyes at her casually questioned faith.

She put her hand on his. "Don't you ever wonder? Like the composer—who was it?—who said he was driven by a music he could never quite hear?"

God, for Ned, had been planted as firmly in the heavens as the yellow sun in a child's drawing. He could see God, or the idea of Him, hovering over his town like the deepest blue rim of atmosphere, the edges indefinable, but there. The idea that she might not see such a thing, or her own imagination's equivalent, terrified him for a moment. He felt it, looking at her quiet smile, unable to respond, thinking of the years they had sat in the same pew at First Methodist, and how he had taken comfort from that too, the ritual, the knowledge that they had done everything anyone would expect to receive God's mercy now.

The necklace still in his hand, he remembered this. He couldn't think of a substitute, couldn't spend too much time looking around or Dobi would know he had not told the truth. He had not realized until this moment, that when Martha had asked him to bury her with the necklace, he had silently refused. If he outlived her, he would have to relinquish her. But he wouldn't give up anything else.

To keep it also seemed absurd, and it wasn't possible to give it to one daughter without causing calculations between them. He found an empty, newer velvet box and slid the chain into the card's two notches, so that it hung in a little "V." He closed it with a muffled click, and Martha sighed in her sleep. He put away the jewelry box and closed the wardrobe and slipped quietly from the room.

Dobi was drying dishes when he came back into the kitchen. When he handed it to her, she seemed surprised by the box more than what was inside it, he thought. She shook her head, confused.

"Go ahead," he said. He felt shaky, even giddy, as with the first time he'd given it.

Dobi opened the box, bent her head to look at the necklace. She touched the pearl with her fingertip. Then she looked up at him smiling, but it was an apologetic smile. "Mr. Dawson, I can't take this."

"I want you to have it."

"I think—" she stopped, took a breath. "Ms. Martha showed it to me once. I know what you mean to do, and I thank you, but it don't have to be that."

She had saved him. She could have rightly claimed offense, pointing both to his lie about buying something and to his disloyalty to his wife, but she didn't. She acted as if she hadn't heard what he'd said before about buying something just for her.

He bowed his head as she closed the box. He had bought it less than a mile away, at Stimson's Jewelers. He had kissed Martha after draping it gently around her bare collar bones. He was surprised, now, to realize that he was crying when Dobi put the box in his hand. The tears rolled down his nose and hit his leather loafers. He felt as if he could lie down on the linoleum, in the worn spot where they now stood. He felt as if he was seeing his life, his time on trains and in conference rooms, in leather chairs around dark wood tables, all designed to lend importance to meetings where numbers were debated and agreed upon, while his wife faded and his daughters lived their own lives. He'd been gone so much that he wasn't needed at all; they had gone on without him.

Dobi put her arms around him, and he was too grieved to be surprised. Maybe she made love to him to forgive him, there on the guest room bed, while Martha slept across the hall. Maybe, he thought later, had she been a few years older, she would've realized that there were plenty of sad old white men in the world, crying over their losses—wives, money, some perceived status—and that these old men would believe that, because they'd had more, they'd lost more than other people. She might have known how to comfort him without giving herself. He was sorry for it, sorry he had taken.

Later, after Dobi had dressed and made the bed and left him sleeping, he'd found the velvet box on the counter where he'd set it. He'd slipped it back into the hand-painted jewelry box. He showered before kissing his wife goodnight.

MARTHA DIED TWO MONTHS LATER, and Dobi spent six nights a week at the house as usual until the final night, and during that time, they did not speak of what had happened. Ned attempted to apologize the next day, but Dobi had pretended not to hear him, and then had asked if he would go to the pharmacy for more morphine or call the doctor to have it delivered.

Dobi told him she was pregnant when she came to clean up after the funeral. It was winter, the rain distinguishable from the low gray sky only by its sound on the windows and bushes outside, quiet tapping.

He had offered her a job coming once a week to do laundry and clean. The way she'd answered him—those two simple words—

without any further explanation, made it clear what this news should mean to him. And then he could see it, the way Martha's apron with the yellow ruffled edging puckered at her waist, the green-and-yellow flowers drawn tighter. Martha had made it from a faded bedsheet, doubling it so that the flowers on the inner ply showed through, shadows of the front pattern. The apron was as old as his daughters, maybe older. He had been standing in almost this exact spot in the kitchen, just home from work, when Martha had told him of her own first pregnancy, which had ended in miscarriage.

A collar of panic tightened around his throat. He wondered if Dobi's mother had known Dobi was pregnant when they'd come to the funeral home during visiting hours. He figured she'd had to have known, but when he searched his memory for any expression or gesture on her part that might have indicated it, he could remember nothing. He had barely paid attention to anything, letting his daughters handle all the arrangements, all the greetings.

He watched as Dobi placed two cardboard boxes on the kitchen table next to a laundry basket full of clothes pulled from Martha's dresser drawers. There were her slips, nightgowns, the pastel jersey tops that he hadn't seen in years. He pretended for a moment that he did not understand the reason she was telling him. "What will you do?" he asked, as one might ask any unmarried young woman who was "in trouble." He knew abortions could be had. Or perhaps she would give it up for adoption. Or perhaps she would miscarry, as Martha had the first time, and he felt a mean stab in his stomach for hoping it.

"What I been doing," she said. She was folding Martha's winter sweaters now. Why had she come back? he wondered. He assumed she was there to ask for money, an ongoing stipend. He would pay what she asked, he decided. "Staying down with my parents," she said then, as if to clarify what continuing in her previous life might mean. There was an edge to her voice that he had not heard before, the tone of a woman who had determined her future.

She turned away from him then, and crouched to retrieve a box mothballs from under the sink, and he knew she didn't want him to ask anything more. She would finish that day and carry his wife's clothes to the Salvation Army in her father's truck when he came back to pick her up, and he would not see her again.

But now that it seemed clear she wouldn't ask him for anything, he wanted to express some kind of concern. "How do you feel?" he asked.

She rose to her feet again, mothball box in hand. "As good as can be," she said, turning to him, lips pressed into a line, and what he saw in her eyes was sadness and a kind of sympathy, which he did not understand, since it was her life that had been carved as clean as the table edge she leaned on.

BUT IT WAS A SMALL TOWN. He heard from Clark the yard man first. Clark was white, retarded—you could see it in the open-mouthed slowness of his thought before words came, or when he poured gasoline in the mower, waiting until long after the container emptied to lift it from the spout. "People say a white man sired him," he said, his gaze sliding from Ned's face to his trembling fingers as he tore a match from a book, striking carefully to light his cigarette. Ned watched the slow progress in horrified silence. Clark raised his head again, blew out smoke. "But that nigger boy's as dark as his mama."

Ned had come out to pick up his paper. He squeezed the roll in his hand, the newsprint soft with late summer humidity. "Why are you telling me this?" He watched Clark's face carefully, trying to read the older man's twitching face as he dragged on his cigarette.

"She worked for you, is all," he said. "Thought you'd wanta know that's why she ain't showing up no more."

Ned thought the man was sincere. He hoped it. His heart squeezed in his ribs; every breath felt like a gasp. "She stopped coming here after Martha died."

Clark bowed his head again, nodding, and Ned was conscious of his pale ankles showing below the hem of his pajamas. "That's fine," he said, as Clark mumbled some form of apology for forgetting—his memory had never been good—and then he patted the man's sweaty shoulder, his own shoulders shaking. "That's all right," he said, before turning back to his silent house.

HE DID NOT SLEEP WELL when he wasn't on the road. His house seemed sealed off, breezeless that fall, even with all the windows open. His daughters invited him to meals, sending him home with casseroles, bread wrapped in wax paper. They never stayed long when they visited.

He began driving past Dobi's house in the early mornings, after he'd been awake for hours but the gray light was just beginning to reveal a slumping screen or the crazed pattern of sun-aged paint. He knew where she lived because he had taken her home on a couple of occasions if her father couldn't get out of the fields during harvest.

What made him finally stop his car was being seen. He'd come later than usual on a Saturday morning, driving slowly from the train station. An old woman sitting on her porch across the road from Dobi's house stopped her work, a knife poised over the white potato flesh in her hand. He felt her eyes on him as he parked next to a ditch and crossed the patchy yard to knock on the door.

He realized as Dobi opened the door that he had brought nothing for her. It seemed he should have brought something. It was the kind of thing Martha would have remembered, and his face burned, thinking of what Martha might do, knowing why he was there.

He tried to think of what to say as Dobi regarded him from the other side of the screen. By then, only the pines held any green, sunlight slanting almost white through bare branches, and, behind them, the yellow glare of field. Through the blur of screen mesh, her unmoving face looked like a photograph. Finally, she opened the door. "He's sleeping," she said. Her face was softer, her hair smoothed back into a bun at the nape of her neck instead of the girlish braids she'd worn the last time he'd seen her. It had been nearly a year. He thought she looked five years older but somehow more beautiful.

"I'm retiring this year," he said, just to have something to say as he sat in the arm chair Dobi had indicated. "Forty years in, nearly, and they told me it was time."

Dobi sat across from him on a bedsheet-covered couch, the pattern like one of Martha's aprons. He wondered for a moment if she'd kept anything. He had buried Martha in the pearl necklace and her wedding band after all. He had kept the engagement ring, and neither of his daughters had asked for it yet. He figured it was just a matter of time before they did—for that and the other jewelry still closed in the dark wardrobe.

Dobi asked after his family and he nodded. "They're fine. Elizabeth's pregnant with her third. Causing quite a stir." As soon as he heard himself, he wished he hadn't said anything about it. He wondered where Dobi's parents were—her father's truck was gone; he wouldn't have stopped otherwise. He imagined her mother in one of the dark back rooms, listening.

Dobi nodded. She straightened the tatted lace doily on the coffee table between them. Finally, she said, "People are going to ask why you're here." Her eyes flicked to meet his and for that moment she looked like the girl who had proved smart enough to be a nurse, quick and capable. Then she looked back to the doily, and it seemed she had nothing more to say to him, now that she had warned him.

He wanted to say that perhaps he'd long overestimated his life, his standing in town and in church, because these days he didn't feel as if he had much ground to lose. What would be the effect if people did know? His own daughters regarded him as a responsibility; his boss, younger than he, masked pity in statements of admiration for his years of service. Sometimes he looked at his hands to make sure he could still see them.

Then, in one of those darkened bedrooms, the boy cried out. Dobi stood as her mother appeared in the hallway, holding the squirming child, who was wrapped in a blue blanket. "He hungry," she said, and Dobi did not say a word as she took the boy from her mother and left the room, closing a door behind her.

Her mother nodded to him. It was a respectful nod, asking Dobi's leave, but also a goodbye. He realized, from her hands clasped at her waist, that she hoped he would not return, and as he replaced his hat and left, he felt sure he would not.

BUT HE CAME BACK THE FOLLOWING SPRING, when the boy was six months old. Alfred was babbling on his grandmother's lap when Dobi let him in. He chose a work day this time, wanting to be sure to avoid the father.

For Christmas he had sent a toy truck made of red-painted metal, with a steering wheel which actually turned the rubber wheels. He'd never bought toys for his daughters; that had been Martha's department since she was around them more and could better assess what they wanted or needed.

If he'd had sons, he might have shopped for them on his travels. But dolls were dolls. The truck had thrilled him; he'd driven it on the living room carpet, carving narrow-gauge circles in the pile.

"What's this?" Nelda had asked, pointing at the carpet, when she came the following afternoon to dust and clean.

"Beats me," he'd said, turning from her gaze.

He packed the truck in a brown box with a twenty-dollar bill and mailed it from the next town, where no one would recognize the address. After that, he sent twenty a month. He didn't know what it cost to feed and clothe babies anymore. It was something.

The truck was perhaps what gained him an audience the following spring. He saw it on the mantle, gleaming, spotless, the morning Dobi let him in. Her mother was an older, smaller version of Dobi, branch-colored lines at the corners of her eyes, which were brown with a hint of yellow-green. She smiled at him and offered coffee.

"Yes, thank you," he said.

She handed the boy to Dobi, who reached for the truck on the mantle. "He likes it," Dobi said. She had two lines starting around her eyes, just like her mother.

He told her about his retirement party. "They held it at the VFW and gave me a plaque," he said. He laughed and shook his head. "Got it in my sock drawer now."

"You should hang it," Dobi said. She looked down at the boy, who was tugging on her collar. Then the boy twisted in Dobi's lap and leaned toward Ned, arm outstretched.

"He wants my pen," Ned said. He was still in the habit of slipping one in his shirt pocket before going out. He held out his hands. Dobi looked at them for an instant, as if not knowing what he was asking, but then she let him take the boy.

He had held Elizabeth's newborn girl a few days before. This had been what prompted him to come, that warm weight in his hands. The boy reached immediately for the pen. Dobi made a noise as if to stop him. "He won't hurt anything," Ned said. Clark had been right; the boy was as dark as his mother. But he had Ned's mouth. Having dragged the pen from Ned's pocket, he brought it, clutched in both fists, to his thin lips and grinned. Ned held the pen back from the child's mouth with one finger. "He's got two teeth," he said, and Dobi smiled proudly, her reserve slipping for a moment.

Her mother was just bringing the coffee when they both froze and turned toward a sound on the gravel road. It was a truck, slowing to pass Ned's parked car. Ned could not even tell its color through the breeze-shifted curtains, but when Dobi and her mother looked at each other, he knew who it had to be. Dobi reached for the child, saying he needed to be changed. Dobi's mother stood in the doorway to the kitchen, facing him, but he knew she wanted somewhere else to go, too. Ned decided he had no choice but stay right where he was. He burned his mouth taking too large a sip of his coffee as he heard the scrape of boots out front. He put down the coffee and stood when Dobi's father came in. He knew the man's Christian name of course; it was customary for a white man to address a colored man of any age as such, but Ned chose to say nothing more than "Afternoon." He did not smile or extend his hand; the normal niceties seemed at that moment more of an offense. He wondered if someone had alerted Dobi's father of his visit, or if the only preparation he'd had was seeing the car parked at the edge of the yard.

Dobi's father wore thick trousers and a jacket zipped to his throat. He held a pair of work gloves and a billed hat in one hand. He was taller than Ned, but narrower, and Ned realized Dobi had gotten her height from him. Dobi's father ducked his head, as if to make up for the difference in their height, and when he spoke to Ned, he looked only in his direction, not straight at him. "I was sorry to hear about Mrs. Dawson."

Ned looked at his polished dress shoes. Even in death, Martha had saved him. "I didn't deserve her."

"We don't know what we deserve." He switched the gloves and hat to his other hand, asked his wife for a couple of water jars. "I'll be outside," he said, nodding to Ned again, leaving the door cracked behind him. Dobi's mother was already clattering in the kitchen, then bustling past him with the empty jars. She came back in quickly, glancing toward the back rooms. If she had sat, Ned would have, too, but she remained standing.

"She gonna have a time with that baby," she said, as if to herself. Then she looked up at Ned, and said, as if to explain, "He never wants to sleep. Child's worried he might miss a single second."

HE STAYED AWAY A WHILE AFTER THAT, but sent money every month and visited every six or so. He knew nothing would be said if he stopped. He had not been held accountable in any way. Not a word had been said to him, no rumors reported. But the thing he had not expected or feared happened. He loved the boy. He thought about him daily, wondered what he might be doing. On a visit the spring after Alfred turned three, he asked Dobi if he could take him fishing. She was cutting a dress of red calico. She had put on some weight, which she carried in her hips, like her mother. She looked up at him from the kitchen table, straight pins pressed in her mouth, scissors in her hand. For a moment, he saw her fear, quick as the glint of metal in the afternoon sun as she stabbed the pins into a cushion. She was afraid he would kill the boy. And there would be nothing to be done.

"Dobi," he said. "At night my knees ache so bad I dream I'm running on them. All I want is something to look forward to."

"You have your grandchildren," she said, scissors tight in her fist. She was right. He had five now, all girls. Would the boy have mattered to him if even one of his been a boy? He'd stopped sending toys because, other than the truck, he never saw them on his visits. He wondered if it was because they didn't want to have to explain them, or didn't want to confirm anything that might be said about the boy's parentage.

"I'm his father," he said, coffee bitter in his throat. They looked at each other across the cut cloth, the color deepening to maroon in the lowering sun, the boy yelling outside, running across the yard with a pack of other children. What was said about his blue Buick, which he washed every Saturday, showing up on the edge of their dirt yard once every few months? The boy turned, recognizing the car. He slowed, looking at the house, and then ran faster to catch up. His arms flashed as fast as the spokes of a turning wheel.

Dobi set the scissors on the table and told him when he could pick the boy up, speaking so quietly he could barely hear her.

SUMMERS THEY WENT TO BASEBALL GAMES in Pendleton or fishing. If it was too wet or cold, he took Alfred to one roadside diner where there was a sympathetic waitress. He always went in first to make sure she was there. The first time, with Alfred waiting in the car, he'd told her the boy was an orphan. It was a necessary lie, but it had pained him, and the waitress had misread it. Her face softened. "What a good Christian you are," she said, her eye following the line of his arm to his ring finger. He still wore his ring then. Her brows drew together in momentary disappointment. "It's through my church," he said, carried away. He always tipped well.

Once, during one of those diner visits, where the boy could eat up to six grilled cheese sandwiches in a sitting, Ned asked what he wanted to be when he grew up.

"A pilot," he'd said. He bit into his sandwich, his pressed fingertips white as the bread.

Ned watched the rain slide down the windows like grease. "You've got to do well in school for that," he'd said, and nothing more.

The boy always addressed him formally—"Mister" or "Sir." But on that occasion, he watched Ned sip his coffee, a question in his eyes. "Who are you?" he'd asked.

"Just an old man," Ned said.

"But who are you?" The boy was six then, and trying to put things together.

"You mean my name?" He said it, surprised.

The boy looked up at the stained ceiling and laughed. "I mean, are you my cousin?"

Ned looked down at his coffee. He could see his face reflected in the oily surface, as if far away. "Yes," he said. "Cousin and friend."

Then the boy laughed so hard Ned thought he might choke. But he was fine, and Ned laughed too, until a man in a booth across the room from them turned to look. He was a traveling salesman, Ned could tell from the thick valise on the opposite bench. Ned thought to ask him what he sold; he thought of sharing traveling stories, but then the man fixed a mean smile on Alfred, and Ned touched the boy's arm. Alfred became silent immediately, his laughter fading to blank watchfulness like a television unplugged, and Ned knew the boy understood more than he let on. He was sorry for it, but relieved, because he didn't want to explain.

WHEN DOBI MARRIED, Ned knew he wouldn't see Alfred as much, maybe only rarely, but he was shocked to learn that they'd moved. Not just a few miles down the road, but to the next state in a fast growing area, where the new husband had found a job in construction. It was Dobi's mother who had told him of the wedding plans when he'd stopped by to find only her there, canning in the steaming kitchen. He'd sent extra money that month, and a note saying congratulations. It was her father who informed him, when he came for a visit a month later, that they were gone.

"Where can I?" Ned began. "How should I?"

"Dobi asked me to say you don't need to send nothing," her father said mildly. He stared out past him, as if watching the horizon to gauge what weather might come.

HIS DAUGHTERS HELPED HIM around the house for the next couple of years, then moved him to a nursing home when he fell and broke his hip. He had refused to use a cane even though his knees had gotten so stiff that he toppled easily. The facility had been built to look like an antebellum mansion. The residents were almost all black; the staff was divided—a few black doctors, white and black nurses and attendants.

At first it had been a shock to find himself in such a mix, but he had assumed the role of jovial salesman among them—hearty hellos, polite "Yessirs" and "Yes, ma'ams." In this twilight world where many of his fellow residents were simply waiting to die, the old divisions seemed to have fallen away.

He sat on a rocking chair on the porch each morning and read the paper, every word of it. Almost every day he thought of how for most of his life he'd barely had time to scan the headlines, and he often mentioned this to whomever happened to be nearby while he was reading. He knew he was repeating himself, but it was satisfying somehow, and so he gave into it. He could still drive, and he still had his mind, even if his repetition made people question his faculties. In some way he liked the faltering glances of his daughters when they brought lunch on Sundays after church. He was no longer something to be taken for granted. They watched him carefully, trying to detect some degree of decline. He appreciated the attention.

Collins was her new last name. He'd found this out not long after she'd left, but had not acted on it. Now that he was settled, and had time on his hands, he figured it was time.

He went to the library to find them. The place smelled of ink and glue and mold and reminded him of his school days. His boyhood seemed to be a memory belonging to someone else; something he might have read about.

The librarian set stacks of phone books in front of him to his left; on his right was the stack he'd finished with. He did not believe he was going to die soon, but he did not know how much longer he would be able to drive. He'd found that things you thought were yours could be nipped away, and faster than you'd think. He'd thrown away his plaque, let his daughters divide his household. He kept a picture of his wife on his bedside table, his cane in the corner. He had nothing of Dobi or Alfred except the slip of paper with their address written in his hand in the library, the shaky script of an old man.

Then he studied maps, planning the best route. He decided not to call. He didn't want to be told not to come; he preferred to be turned away at the door, if it came to that, cane and all.

WHEN THE BOY ANSWERED THE DOOR, they knew each other. He had that white man's mouth. Not full, but thin as a newscaster's, with a dip in the middle of his upper lip just like Ned's. The boy was taller than he was. He wore a red T-shirt and tight blue jeans; his hair, wavy, not kinky, rose in a dark cloud from his temples.

"How old are you, now, son?" Ned asked, smiling at their mutual recognition. He wasn't as nervous as he'd thought he'd be. He felt triumphant, actually. The old rhythms of the road had come back to him; the smell of bleach in motel sheets, the paper-wrapped cakes of soap. He felt clean, even after a day of driving with the windows down.

"Seventeen." The boy's face was long and angular, like his own, but his eyes and nose were Dobi's.

"You still in school?"

The boy stared hard at him. "Which school you mean?"

Ned didn't know what he was being asked. The boy could read his confusion. His smile was a sneer. "They gave the nigger school to the primary kids," he said. "But they're saying no breathing white person gonna let us in that high school."

He was an old man; he could feel it in the weight of his joints; the slowness of his mind. Years before, the salesman in him would have been ready with a friendly comment or joke to take the edge off the moment. *I'm your father*, he wanted to say. A father at fifty-eight, and then not a father. Not held as such, to his relief. A price for that, though, even so. "I didn't come here for a lesson, son," he said, a sudden rage thick in his throat.

The boy laughed at him. He laughed so hard he had to bend over, or made a show of doing so. But even in such contempt, he sounded joyful.

"Who's there?" Ned heard Dobi say. Then she was at the door, stepping around Alfred's still doubled form. Her hair was cut short and turned under at the edges, professional. She wore a suit jacket and skirt, and stood his height in her stocking feet. Even in the cloudy afternoon light, he could see in Dobi her mother's lines, her mother's skin. She was shaken, recognizing him, eyes tight in her sockets.

The boy stopped laughing. "Who are you, to come here?"

Ned leaned on his cane under that stare. He didn't have time, standing on that stoop, in that middle-class neighborhood with its reasonable rows of houses, to explain his regret. Or to admit that he didn't like a black man to look him in the eye, even his own son, and being completely honest would require such an admission, he knew. Or to plead that he had tried to be a good man within the confines of his life, or to say that he even believed sometimes that he had been good. He could only look back at that stare, that firm, familiar mouth.

"Your mother," he said, finally. "She told me I would always be welcome." He tried to meet her eyes, to plead with her, but she turned away from him. He was saying a prayer now, not the truth. He could almost convince himself that at some point over the years, she had voiced an invitation. He believed he could hear it, even now, as he lowered himself painfully to his knees.

Jimmy the Brain
and the Beautiful Aideen

I MET AIDEEN ON MY FIRST NIGHT working at Mike's Beer Mart—
Mike was her husband. A freak October storm had iced
everything over. I was stocking Schlitz when Aideen pulled into
the drive-through. Their three kids were in back, the littlest in her
car seat, the boys strapped in on either side, their sock-feet kicking
the seatbacks. Mike came around the counter to greet them. "Don't
let the kids out, hon, it's too cold," he said, and Aideen shook her
head and winked at me, as if to say he didn't give her much credit.
I liked her right away.

Mike hooked a thumb toward me. "He's going to do nights."
While he leaned in the back windows to hug the boys, I introduced
myself. I'd just started an hour before—I'd gone a different way
home from campus, and when I stopped in, Mike had asked me
did I want to earn some extra cash.

"Well, what do you think?" Aideen asked me, eyebrows raised
and lips pressed into a grin that said she wasn't all that concerned
about my opinion. The place had been a body shop before. You
could see where the hydraulic lifts had been ripped out and the
holes filled with fresh concrete. It had rear and front metal garage
doors. Instead of coming around to an outside service window,
customers drove inside, where they could load their own cars if
they wanted and pay at the counter. But Mike had told me we
should always offer to load for them. "Service, man," he'd said.
"That's how we'll take over around here." There was a large beer

53

and wine cooler on one side of the drive-through and smaller coolers for pop on the other. The twenty-proof liquor, the strongest stuff we were allowed to sell, he kept behind the counter along with the cigarettes.

"Looks fine to me," I said to Aideen. My father was laid off from Diebold and my mother stood in the kitchen a lot, washing dishes and whispering on the phone with her friends about who'd gotten the latest pink slip. Worry drew up her eyebrows like a bad facelift. As far as I was concerned, a job was a job.

Aideen was about to ask me something else when a guy came around the corner and pulled in behind her too fast, his tires squealing on the concrete as he braked. Mike straightened up, looking at him. Aideen checked him out in her rearview.

"You work here?" the guy yelled at Mike. He inched his car toward Aideen's bumper, bouncing the brakes.

"With you in a minute," Mike said, keeping his eyes on the guy an extra second before turning back to Aideen. The baby had started crying.

Aideen's eyes flicked back to her rearview again. "Don't forget the deposit," she said.

Mike leaned to kiss her but stopped short; she was already rolling. I went to get the King Cobra that the guy yelled for, and when he paid and pulled out, tires squealing again, Mike and I watched his headlights swing across the asphalt. In the silence afterward, I thought I could hear the ice expanding in the cracks, buckling the road.

But those first few weeks after the storm and before winter really set in were pretty nice. A chilly night breeze blew out the fumes, but you didn't even have to zip your coat to stay warm. The sky out front turned pink in the evening, and even though there wasn't a tree or a strip of green anywhere—across the street it was just a Quick Stop and a Wendy's—those sunsets made everything look better. There was a steady stream of customers, and Mike and Aideen always gave me free beer. I thought they had a pretty good gig going.

I worked with Aideen a lot because the rule was two people working the counter, and never more than one woman. Two men was ideal. When Aideen had to work, Mike scheduled me with her, because, as he said, "You're level-headed, not like most guys your age." He only had maybe ten or eleven years on me, but I guess he saw it in those terms: He was in one camp, and you were in another—and if you didn't know the difference, well, he did.

But then I pulled the same thing with Aideen a couple of weeks after I started. We'd figured out we were exactly ten years apart, same birthday even: October fifth, which had just passed. Without thinking, I said, "I can't believe you're that much older."

I meant that she looked my age. I still hate to think of it, how she looked at me and then, realizing what I'd meant, started laughing. "Ten years is nothing," she said. "You'll see."

Then she told me about meeting Mike at Michigan State in the fall of 1980. It came down to a decision between two post-game parties, her roommate convincing her to go to one instead of the other. Mike and Aideen knew each other from high school, but meeting again in a new place triggered something between them, was how Aideen put it, and they fell in love. They stayed together even after Mike flunked out and had to live with his parents for a while, selling used cars, and for the next three years she finished school while he saved money for a big Ohio-style wedding—ten bridesmaids and groomsmen, the big banquet room at the downtown Holiday Inn—which her father could've paid cash-out-of-wallet for. But Mike was trying to prove himself because Aideen's father, a semi-retired Diebold exec, was none too happy about Aideen marrying Mike, even though Mike was from the right side of town and a former football player.

"We're used to sticking it out," she said then, and she looked over the counter as if the Beer Mart was just another example. She was about as beautiful as anyone I'd ever seen in person—long, almost-black hair, pale skin, and almond-shaped brown eyes, but also a roundness in her face that made her look soft and young.

And she had a good head for business as far as I could tell. The Beer Mart might have been Mike's idea, but she made things happen. She got a lottery machine through her father's connections, which probably pissed Mike off, but it brought in more business. And she ordered a big red neon sign to make the place stand out better from the road.

But when it was time to count the take and lock up, and I walked her to her car, she said, "Race you to Thirtieth." That's where the line was, where the streets got cleaner, the old Victorians a row of white cakes, no sagging, no rot. I saw it in her face, dashboard-lit and determined, how she gunned it out of the lot. She really was racing.

My family and I lived just over the line on Thirty-Second. She and Mike lived further north in a bungalow at the edge of the richest neighborhood, where her parents lived. At that end of town, there's a pathetic, half-mile-wide lake where people ride their motorboats in tight circles during the short summers. There's a bar behind the docks with dark paneling and the usual mounted fish. This is what's known as The Club. Aideen told me she'd had her graduation party there; she was laughing, embarrassed, and I have to admit I wished I could've been there, but I knew I wouldn't have been invited anyway, even if I had been her age.

That winter was cold. Probably no worse than normal, but I felt almost every night of it, working with those huge open garage doors. Mike hung a space heater above the counter with chicken wire and jumper cables, which didn't do much except burn your scalp if you were tall, like me. It was fine for Aideen, and even for Mike. He'd reach up and try to tilt the metal grill of the heater to warm us better. He'd say, "These are the kinks you gotta work out in the first year of business."

One night he told me how he'd gotten it started. "See, I paid attention," he explained. "There were drive-throughs all over town, especially by the campus, but not around here. The civic center's two blocks away and we're not far from downtown."

This seemed sharp to me at the time, but maybe Mike didn't notice how, behind the main drag, the rows of houses looked like crumpled paper. There was a halfway house in one direction and, sure, the civic center in the other, but those people bought their drinks inside, and when they left they headed north as fast as they could.

But Mike wanted to think of himself as a businessman, and he wanted to impress Aideen's father, who really was a businessman, and after a while he convinced Aideen to talk to her father about some start-up money, even though she didn't like the idea of a drive-through because of safety. He told me about meeting the old man in his study, showing him plans of how people could drive around the back and pick out their own booze inside, out of the weather, and exit the front. He showed where the beer, pop and liquor would go, and how there would eventually be a wine room.

"I was nervous, right?" Mike said. "I had all these papers and figures, but after selling cars you know how to close a deal." We were standing at the glass doors of the self-service beer cooler, pulling out cases and loading them into a friend of mine's trunk. I had talked up the place, how cheap it was, and word had gotten around. "So what's the old bastard do?" Mike continued. "He gives me this big sneer and says, 'What're you going to call it, Mike's Beer Mart?' And I just smiled right back at him and said, 'That's what I'll call it.' So what could he say? There I was, taking his advice."

Mike went behind the counter to ring up the beer and I counted up the cases and took the cash. I checked the beer cooler to make sure we had the stock displayed that the regulars liked—forty-ouncers like Laser, Magnum and Colt 45 (notice a theme, here?)—and when I came back, Mike was sitting on a stool with his feet balanced on the counter to get them closer to the heater. "This works pretty good," he said, and he seemed proud of himself, having figured that out.

My father knew who Aideen's father was and he hated that I was working for people who'd laid him off. "You can't think of anything better than selling liquor to poor shits?" he said when I took the job. But he wasn't in much of position to judge, staring at the television as the unemployment checks ran out. I thought of saying he should take his own advice. Running a snow truck paid pretty well, even if it was seasonal, but it would've gotten us through that winter a lot better than his ass in the Barca Lounger. I could have said that and he knew it, but neither one of us wanted those words between us with my mother in the kitchen trying to figure out something new to do with discount ground burger. My sisters could scream and cry at him over anything, but the tension between him and me ran deep, and there wasn't room for argument. That spring he got hired back on, and then he got laid off again not long after, but he was so close to retirement by then that they called it an early package, something the union cooked up to save face. And he did pick up some shifts at the Home Depot after that because, he liked to tell everyone, he got his tools on discount.

"I'm a trooper." That's what Aideen said one day after she found out Mike hadn't paid the cigarette bill. When the rep came to for the POS racks she just paid him out of the till. After he left, she stood there staring at the salt-white road. Then she asked me if I'd been paid for the week.

I hadn't, but I didn't want to press the point if she'd just gotten cleaned out with the cigarette bill. Besides, I gave most of the money to my mother so my father wouldn't know I was helping. I shrugged, and she handed me fifty dollars. "That's right, isn't it?"

"You don't have to—"

"And you don't have to play hero, now. No one's asking you to volunteer here." She shook my shoulder as if to say *snap out of it.* "You want a beer?"

Pabst was on tap that day. She cracked open two cans and handed one to me. She asked me how school was going and I told her I was trying to figure out whether I should look for a job as soon as I got my teacher's certificate or go to grad school and then maybe qualify for higher pay. If I didn't get a job right away, my father wouldn't understand it. Or worse, maybe my mother wouldn't.

"You know what?" she said. "You should feel lucky that you have all that ahead of you. I mean, I'm kind of jealous."

We leaned on the counter and sipped our beers. I didn't know what it felt like to get to a place in life and realize I was going to be there for a while, happy or not. But I did know one thing. I liked being shoulder to shoulder with Aideen. I liked being with her more than anything else I had going in my life.

I was trying to think of something to say to impress her when in walked this guy who I figured had to be from the halfway house. He was tall, big-boned, but even in his two or three coats, you could see how skinny and bent he was, especially right around the shoulders, as if the gravity got worse up there with that overlarge head. He had white hair though I noticed later his face was smooth as a boy's.

He shuffled in about halfway to the counter, but when he saw Aideen, he stopped. Just stood in the middle of the drive-through, staring like he'd never been in a chopped-up warehouse or seen a woman before. I imagined a comic book thought-bubble over his head saying something like "Wowza!" with stars and comets exploding around him.

"Hi," he said to her finally. I could have been invisible.

"Hi," she said back. She knew right away what was going on. A woman like Aideen probably got those looks all the time, maybe not always that straightforward, but she was graceful about it. She smiled at him like he was any other customer, even though his sneakers were untied and the coat he was wearing under his ski jacket, which was so small he couldn't come close to zipping it, was magenta wool and probably a woman's.

"I'm Jimmy the Brain," he said, or really, "Jimmy d'bwain" was how it came out because of some speech impediment he had. You could see how someone with a skull like his might get called Brain, a cruel twist since he must have been retarded. Which was probably why the nickname didn't bother him.

"Can I help you?" I said, using my friendly-but-firm classroom voice developed during field work.

He glanced at me just long enough, it seemed, to make sure I was really there, then dismissed me, shuffling closer to Aideen. He came all the way to the counter, which we had been leaning against. Aideen backed off. I wanted to protect her, or at least look like I could.

"What can I get you?" I said loudly, the way people yell at foreigners, like the extra volume will translate the English for them all of a sudden.

He shook his head as if to wave away the sound I'd made. It was a quick movement, eyes closed, the motion of someone trying to get back his concentration, but with him it looked drunken, and I inhaled the heater-dried air between us, trying to smell alcohol.

He opened his eyes, looked at Aideen, and put his palms on the counter as if to steady himself. "Dr. Pepper, please, lady," he said. He wasn't trying to be rude, I knew right then. He said lady because that's what she was to him, in the classic sense—she was a lady and he was a peasant, and he was fine with that.

I went around the counter and brought him a sixteen-ounce plastic bottle of Dr. Pepper from the pop cooler.

"You got it in a can?" Still looking at her, not me, as if the bottle had just appeared next to him.

Aideen shook her head. "I'm sorry. Well, in the machine we do," she said, pointing to the drink machine next to the pop cooler. "But this is a better deal."

"It's okay it's okay," he said, shaking his heavy head again, the stalk of his neck bent under it. He pulled change from a pocket and scattered it on the table. He didn't have enough.

"Looks like you need about thirty more cents plus tax," I said, partly to be helpful and partly to dig him for ignoring me.

He grabbed his ears and shook his head hard, as if the sound of my voice was now a painful irritation. He slapped the counter and turned around, his back to us. "Oh no, oh no," he said.

"Maybe you have some more in your pockets?" I said.

He turned and glared at me then, focusing on me like a man about to shoot. It pissed me off, and I was ready to haul him out of there. Even if he had an inch or two on me, I was going to give him a good run. "I don't. Have it," he said to me.

Aideen reached under the counter. "Maybe I have it," she said. I reached across the counter and grabbed her hand so she wouldn't get her purse out. That seemed to be asking for it, and it was the first moment I'd felt a little vulnerable there. Here was this crazy guy getting upset, and who knew what he had hidden in all those layers. I dug in my jeans pockets and pulled out two quarters, dropped them on the counter. "That'll cover it," I said.

He nodded his head, stepped back from the counter and stepped toward it again, a shuffling dance, gripping his Dr. Pepper hard around the neck. "Rich man," he said to the counter, but he meant me. That's what fifty cents had bought me. I bit my lip to keep from laughing—I didn't want him getting worked up again now that it looked like we might finally get rid of him. "Rich man," he said again. Then, "What's your name?" to Aideen.

She told him, and he closed his eyes, as if he could feel her voice roll over him.

"The Beautiful Aideen," he said in his slurry, flat tone, and yet the words seemed filled with emotion. And that's what he called us every time he saw us after that.

There were other guys from the halfway house, too. There was James who wore a patch and claimed he'd gone through a plate glass window when he was a kid—someone had hit his mother's car and he'd lost an eye, and he said she'd gotten a big payout because it had happened at a bank. He begged cigarettes. "She's loaded," he said. "Call her, just call her and she'll pay." He gave us a different number every time. We kept a pack open just for him and doled them out. And there was small-framed Willie, who was a lot younger than the others—smooth, coffee-colored skin and bright eyes that seemed focused and sane when he looked at you, and I had hopes that maybe someday he'd make it on his own, even though he smoked cigarette butts he found on the street and tried to trade potholders he'd woven in craft class for beers. To me that was at least enterprising.

Then there were the guys in low-slung cars; they were practically lying down at the wheel, prison tattoos on their biceps like bruises under their thin T-shirt sleeves, the dark gleam of their pieces on the floorboards. Every time I worked with Aideen I expected them to rob us, but they didn't. Maybe it's because we always spotted them with extra change if they said they were short, or maybe they just felt sorry for us—they could see before we did that the place was going to fail. They'd order their Mad Dog, Brass Monkey or Thunderbird, and sometimes they were already so messed up I wondered if we should sell them anything more. One Saturday night when I was working with Mike, I called out to him, indicating with my eyes a customer who'd just pulled around in a dented Trans-Am. His head bobbed on his neck like an infant's. Mike was behind the counter. For some reason, Aideen was there, too; the kids were with her parents. Maybe they thought a weekend night would be busy, though we hadn't had many customers at all. Mike nodded. "Go ahead," he said.

I walked over to pick the bottles, but when I turned around, Aideen shook her head at me. I was standing there in the bay, in between the car and the counter. The guy dangled his arm out his window, cash pinched in his hand. I moved to block his view of her. "He's too drunk," she mouthed.

Mike held up his hand, palm out, to stop her. "Do it," he said to me.

After the guy left, Aideen mumbled something about getting sued, but Mike pretended not to hear. Then she said she was going to pick up some burgers. She wouldn't look at either of us when she left.

Mike watched her drive off. He lit a cigarette and shook his head. "If they want to kill themselves, who are we to stop them?"

By then, it was the middle of winter, though not officially—it was only mid-December. But I can't seem to remember any daylight from that time. I was either in the basement of the education building or out in that black cold at the Beer Mart, my hands stiff and my face raw. I started sipping whiskey from a bottle they kept under the counter to loosen the muscles in my back. I noticed Aideen was drinking a lot more, too. I mean really drinking. Not just having a few beers when business was slow, which seemed to be more and more often, but breaking out a bottle of vodka and mixing it with a 7-Up. She usually had a solid buzz on by the time we had to close.

"You okay to drive?" I asked her as we walked out one night, not long before Christmas.

Aideen leaned against her salt-crusted blue Ford Taurus. Gray, truck-shoveled snow lined the parking lot like a low stone wall. Headlights washed across her face, and I turned to look—it was after midnight, and she had the bank bag. The car backed out again, someone lost and turning around.

"Let's go somewhere," she said.

"Where?" I said. I felt a tightness in my chest that was partly nerves and partly hope. At that point in my life I never would've thought I'd be attracted to a woman with three kids, but then I'd never been around a woman like Aideen, day after day. I wanted an up-against-the-car grinding kiss with her, and then I wanted to be a gentleman and say no, to show my loyalty to Mike. I had this movie in my head.

"How about Louie's?" she said. She unlocked her car, tossed the bank bag and her purse into the car seat in back, and leaned across the front seat to unlock my side.

I rounded my back and clamped my shoulders down to keep from shivering against the cold passenger seat. I would have driven but I had an unheated truck, a winter beater. I could have offered to drive her car since I'd only had a couple beers and not much whiskey and I was definitely the more sober one, but I was afraid that if I suggested it, she might change her mind and just head home.

When we were driving, Aideen asked, "Do you think we choose what happens to us?" The question surprised me, because I figured any woman from one of the richest families in town with a husband and kids and a business had done a fair amount of choosing. I had a feeling that even though she was talking out loud, she wasn't talking to me. Then she brought up Mike, though she never said his name. "Like, if you fell in love with someone one day, would you fall in love with them the next week?"

"I don't know," I said. I felt that twinge of hope again in my chest. Until then, she'd talked about Mike only terms of the business, like when he'd bounced a check, and even then she'd never really criticized him. I wanted to believe she might have picked me over him if the timing had been different. "I think we do what we want."

I don't believe that anymore. But right then I was saying what I hoped she wanted to hear.

"I think that's a lot of bullshit," she said, and laughed. She lurched the car into a parking spot at Louie's and cut the engine. The place was dead, only a few cars in the lot. "It's so damn cold out there," she said.

I had my hand on the car door, feeling for the handle, when she leaned toward me. I thought she was going to say something, and I turned back to her. I remember the rustle of her ski jacket, which seemed so loud, and then her face was close to mine, and I felt the heat coming off of her skin in the moment before she kissed me. She wasn't tentative, her tongue slipping between my lips, the ripe-fruit alcohol taste strong in my mouth. Her fingers were cold stones on my throat, hunting for my jacket zipper. I dragged it down and folded her against me; she straddled me, and I remember clenching my hands to warm them and to steady myself. They were so cold I worried that if I touched her she'd pull away, but then she reached around and found them and guided them to her breasts. I couldn't seem to get enough air—that ache in the throat—but I was scared to stop kissing her, scared of everything. I was shy with women; I didn't get laid until I was nineteen, a relationship that had taken months to develop, with the girl pushing me along. And that girl had been nowhere as beautiful as Aideen. There in her car, I could barely move. I cupped her breasts so gently I almost wasn't touching them. She grabbed my hands and slid them underneath her sweater, up against her ribs. She opened her bra and leaned forward so that the weight of her breasts pressed into my palms. All the while she was kissing me, shivering, her hips fitted to my groin, and she had to have felt how hard I was. I tried not to think about it. I was going to do whatever she wanted. Everyone's been there, felt that kind of need.

She moved her hands down to my jeans and started working at my zipper. I watched her face as she concentrated on her fumbling fingers. She was too drunk to think about what she was doing and I knew it. But what worried me wasn't the idea of taking advantage of her, and not even of betraying Mike, but that I would lose control and come the moment she touched me. Just the fear of it cooled me down a little.

She got my jeans unzipped and started to slide her hand into my underwear. But then she stopped. She rested her forehead against my neck for a moment. "Tighty-whiteys," she said against my ear with a low chuckle. I felt my face heat. I reached for her waistband, but she rocked back on her hips, evading my fingers. She said, "You get to where you forget what it's like to be wanted like this." I reached for her again and she scooted back on my thighs and pulled her hand away from me. I knew it was over. But I held her, still hopeful, until she slid off my lap. I zipped my jeans, my balls aching, and looked over at her. She'd leaned back against the headrest, staring through the windshield. "I'm sorry," she said. "I'm being stupid."

I was trembling, heart pounding. She said she was sorry again, and I said I wasn't. I told her she was beautiful, and she smiled. "The Beautiful Aideen," she said.

She drove us back to my truck and kissed me on the cheek while we were still in the car. I turned my face to hers, but she pulled back just in time. "Race you to Thirtieth," she said. I got out and watched her shoot across the parking lot, headlights bouncing as she turned onto the street. Then I got in my truck, the vinyl seat ice cold under my ass, and drove home to my dark house and my sleeping parents and sisters. I jerked off in the bathroom like a thirteen-year-old.

I worked with Mike the next night. It was so cold it hurt to breathe through your nose. I was lightheaded with nerves as I walked in from the parking lot.

Inside, I couldn't stop shivering. "You okay?" Mike asked me. I nodded and blew on my hands, standing next to him under the heater. It hadn't occurred to me until that morning to wonder whether Aideen would say anything to him. I hadn't thought about how people got killed over things like that.

"You sure?" He sounded genuinely concerned, but I wondered if he was playing with me. A guy like Mike wouldn't let something like his wife dry-humping another guy just pass without a confrontation. "Get a beer," he said. "Better yet, some of this." He pulled the bottle from under the counter and poured a few fingers for both of us in those plastic cups he sold with keg rentals. He tilted his cup toward mine in a toast and drained it, and I couldn't see anything in his expression except a slackening when the alcohol went down. And I knew right then. She hadn't told him, and that could only mean I might have another chance with her.

I was scheduled to work with Aideen in two nights. I could have rattled off the exact number of hours until I saw her again at any point during those next couple of days. For the first time in my life, I was happy it was winter, so I could keep my coat zipped and hide the perpetual hard on I had from thinking about how I would kiss her, slide my hands under that turtleneck again, and guide her into the cooler, where we'd have privacy but we'd still be able to hear cars coming in. I imagined her laid back on a pallet of twelve packs, her legs around my waist. It didn't bother me in the least to be thinking all this while working right next to her husband.

And for his part, Mike didn't seem to notice how absentminded I was all of a sudden—not only had he not sensed any difference in me, he seemed no different, either.

But when Aideen came in two nights later, it was only to pick up beer and wine. I already knew something was up because Mike was there instead of her. He looked tired, preoccupied, like when the bills came in and he was trying to figure out which ones to pay. For a while, I hoped she was just running late and Mike was covering until she could take over, but after a couple of hours I was starting to feel sick, actually nauseous. I did my best to act casual when I finally asked Mike where she was.

I had just loaded a customer, and Mike was breaking down boxes. He stopped what he was doing and straightened up. Then he turned and looked at me with no expression on his face. "She'll be through in a little bit," he said, in the same flat tone he used with the prison-tattooed customers who came in bouncing their brakes and yelling.

She'll be through. I could have, and should have, walked away right then. It wouldn't have been an apology or an admission. Well, maybe it would have been an admission. But I was as hooked on my hopes—my fantasies—as the drunks who were keeping us open by then. Any worries I had about Mike were nothing compared to my desire to be close to Aideen, if only for a few minutes.

When she rolled in, the kids were in the back seat just like the first time I'd seen her. Mike went around and talked with the older boy; the other two were asleep. He didn't look at me when he went to get the beer. It was like an invitation: Take your chance. And I jumped at it. I came around the counter and rested my forearm on the roof of her car in what I hoped was a relaxed-looking pose. All I could think about was where I had touched her, and of how she had been the one to reach for me first. "How are you?"

"Pretty good," she said. Her face was puffy like when she was hung over, a look that unfortunately had become familiar to me.

But she smiled brightly. It was her customer service smile, not even a hint of conspiracy. "I'm taking the kids down to Sarasota for Christmas." She squeezed the steering wheel, spread her fingers, squeezed again. "We'll be back in a couple of weeks."

I straightened so I could breathe. *We'll be back.* She was a mother in a four-door sedan packed with three kids; she wanted me to understand this.

But I didn't want to accept it. "Leaving kind of early, aren't you? School's not out yet." I knew this, of course, because I had three days of teaching left in my fieldwork, and my sisters were still in school, too. I guess I thought I could argue her out of her plan, with the kids' duffels packed on the floorboard.

She nodded but she didn't answer, just kept looking straight ahead, like she was already driving. *Please*, I wanted to say. Instead, after a moment, I tapped the roof of her car. "Good trip," I said, just as Mike came back with the beer. His chin ticked upward at the sound of my voice. I turned away so neither of them could see my face.

After she left, I waited for Mike to tell me to get the hell out. I wondered if he'd try to kick my ass. I wanted him to, in a way. It would've made what had happened between me and Aideen more real somehow, not something I'd maybe dreamed. But he didn't do either. In fact, he seemed to go back to his old self with me, talking about how he was going to repaint the exterior when the cold let up, and would I want to help with that. He told me Aideen's old man had gotten a toupee. "I guess he wants to blend in better down there in Florida," he said, laughing, inviting me with his eyes to laugh along, too. Maybe he'd decided it wasn't my fault, that a guy "my age" was susceptible, particularly to a woman like Aideen. Maybe it was like a score for him, another man wanting his wife, but he'd shown me she was still his, and he'd sent her away, where she'd stay until he called her back. He had that kind of power. He could afford to joke around with me because I'd never had a chance with her anyway. That was the message, I decided. But in the lulls between customers, I thought about what might change the course of things—a car accident, a robbery. I even found myself wondering if I might help those things along. How would I do it? I figured this was how it started for anyone who decided to claim someone they thought belonged to them. Or should belong. There was a door you walked through, at first just in your thoughts. And then another door, and thoughts became actions. And then later you might ask yourself if you could have chosen any differently. As if it had happened to you rather than because of you.

At the end of that same week, Mike and I were closing up, and I was hanging around, waiting for him to pay me. Then he told me he couldn't. "Things are tight right now, that's all."

I shrugged. I wanted the money of course, but I was actually elated. He was failing, and Aideen would soon see this for herself. She wouldn't let him drag her and the kids down with him. She'd unload Mike before that happened, and then she'd unload the Beer Mart, maybe let the kids stay with her parents while she found a job. And I'd be waiting when she was ready to start again. We'd move away, and these few months before we got together would be nothing more than a dark smudge in our memory. Somehow I never thought about where the kids would figure in.

"That's okay," I said. I pulled on my ski gloves. It was so cold I would've worn them all the time, but you couldn't handle money. It didn't matter; I could hardly feel the cold right then. I might even have been smiling.

He must have seen something in my face, because as I was getting ready to walk out, he asked me, "Do you miss her?"

I stopped. I was glad my back was to him. My shoulders felt tight as wire. "Yeah, sure," I said, not wanting to wait too long to answer, and yet already knowing my answer had given me away. I could've said "Who?" Or cracked some joke. A joke would've saved me. I turned back to him then. I was shaking, almost dizzy. "Don't you?"

Mike slipped the cash bag into his ski jacket and zipped it up, his eyes on me the whole time. "Every day," he said. Then he cut the fluorescent light over the counter. I walked out ahead of him, trying not to go too fast or too slow. I'd always thought it was bullshit when people said, "I could feel him looking at me." But right then, I understood. I could feel his eyes on my back, like a heat spreading. By the time I got to my car, my hands were shaking so hard I had to take my gloves off again to get the keys in the ignition. That time, I really did consider not coming back to work again. But I did, and not just because I needed the money. It was that movie in my head, still playing.

There was a spike in business through the holidays, which got Mike back to talking about putting in the wine room. He started paying me out of the till again, every night if I wanted. I wondered how he kept things straight, but I didn't ask questions. I didn't realize back then that everyone, everyone is flailing. People ignore the obvious. They don't pay the bills and they give out free beers and get up to, say, a quart of vodka a day and believe they can go on like that indefinitely. But then, maybe Aideen didn't really believe that. She just did it anyway.

She got back right after New Year's, but I didn't work with her for several weeks, and I only saw her when she was coming through to pick up booze. The kids were always in the back seat. On one of those stops, she told me she'd had the flu ever since she'd gotten back from Florida. The skin under her eyes was dark. "Anything I can do?" I asked her, leaning into her car again, my pulse thick in my throat. *Anything.* I knew she didn't have the flu. I could smell that too-ripe sweetness rising from her skin, could see the jerkiness in her muscles as she shook her head no. It didn't make me want her any less. And I wanted her to want something from me. "Let me see you," I whispered.

Mike was helping a customer in line behind her, and she kept glancing back in her rearview, just like the first night I'd met her. "I'm fine, sweetie," she said. She patted my hand and looked up at me then, trying to manage that customer service smile. But her lips pressed into a flat line like she was bearing down on a pain. Then she took a deep breath. "I'm a trooper."

By late January, the holiday rush was long gone. Even the drunks seemed to be on the wagon. And the gangsters were pretty scarce, too. When they peeled out, snow spun off their wheels in marbled chunks, which we shoved out to the parking lot with a push broom so it wouldn't melt and then freeze overnight. The only regulars came from the halfway house, but beyond their loose change, all they brought was sad entertainment. Jimmy the Brain, for an example, got nailed for stomping on ketchup packets at the Wendy's across the street. The manager called it in, said he was threatening the customers, who, I could tell from watching their comings and goings across the street, didn't look like they had much more on the ball than Jimmy. But this was a way to get him out of their line of vision. I could understand the temptation. He'd been pestering us earlier until Mike gave him a Dr. Pepper and a Ho-Ho, both of which he ate while crouching behind the Dumpster out back. Then he'd wandered over to the Wendy's, worn out his welcome there, and the next thing I saw was him running in front of traffic, back toward us. A cop car pulled into our lot, and one guy took off after him. Jimmy was laughing and shrieking, arms flapping right until the cop tackled him. He cuffed Jimmy and dragged him back to the car. At one point Jimmy almost made it back onto his feet—he was crab walking, in a kind of limbo, but the cop jerked his cuffed hands toward the sky, and Jimmy's whole body flipped over, so he went the rest of the way on his knees. The last thing I saw was his large head getting clocked on the car door frame.

He came back after a few days and showed off his bruises. He told Mike and me that they'd tried to question him but he'd foiled them because, tapping his temple, he was *Jimmy d'bwain*, and he'd smuggled a video camera into jail with him, and he'd taped the whole thing, and he was going to sue the pants off them, sue the pants off them. We laughed because not to laugh would be to recognize that this was not a joke, that this retarded man as old as my father had been beaten by the cops and thought he was outsmarting them, and this was real.

While Jimmy was on county-sponsored vacation, Mike had me doing inventory, which seemed pretty pointless because there wasn't that much on the shelves. I picked up a dust-covered bottle of sloe gin. "Maybe we should send this stuff back," I said to Mike. He didn't answer right away, and I turned around. He was leaning against the counter, arms folded, watching me. I put the bottle down.

"I need you to work some nights alone, just for a couple of weeks," he said.

I looked away from him, across the counter, at the blank space on the opposite wall where the lottery machine had been; Mike apparently hadn't paid that bill either. The outline of the machine remained; the wall was smudged gray from exhaust fumes after only a few months. I thought of how that stuff had settled on our skin, in our throats.

He saw me looking. "I'm going back to the car lot for a while, to get us through this slump."

I knew that meant Aideen would be staying home with the kids indefinitely. The thought of not seeing her scared me a lot more than sitting on a bunch of booze by myself in a bad neighborhood. But I nodded an okay. I didn't want to be looking for another job when it was too late to get a place on the snow trucks and too early for construction. And somehow I felt I owed it to Mike, and maybe he knew that.

He said, "We just have to make it til it warms up, and people are out again. Graduation parties and shit, right?" He grinned in a not-unfriendly way, but it was a dig at me, since I was only a couple months from finishing. And maybe also at Aideen, and anyone else who'd played around in college while he was selling cars, saving his money for a deejay and a sit-down chicken dinner for two hundred. He might have been fucking up, but he was fucking up in the real world; that was the message.

"Right," I said.

Jimmy the Brain never produced a video tape of his trials, but he did actually have a camera, a Kodak Instamatic X-15—I remember that because he always made a point of saying the whole name. It probably took 110- or 126-sized film cartridges, the kind of camera you might have given to a kid back in the seventies. After he got out of jail, he stopped in nearly every one of those nights I worked alone, clutching his camera, looking for Aideen. He'd walk in far enough to get a view of the counter, then stop when he saw me and turn around and walk off without a word. One night, he came all the way to the counter and bent to rest his forehead on the metal-trimmed edge. His big head rolled side to side. He was crying.

"She's just not here," I said. I could've told him she'd be back any day, even though I didn't know that for a fact, but I didn't feel like I had comfort to spare. Maybe I wanted to punish him, just like the cops, for being who he was, and for wanting her. Or maybe I hated how I'd cried for her too, more than once, up in my room like one of my younger sisters.

"Gimme a deuce," he said then, throwing all his change on the counter. It was the first time he'd ever bought alcohol. I didn't count the money, just handed the bottle over. I watched him lurch away, head jerking, and wondered if I'd see him again.

A couple nights after that, a guy walked in and wandered around, looking in the coolers. I figured he was a new resident from the halfway house.

"You got any Magnum?" he asked finally.

"It's not out there?"

He shook his head, hands in his pockets. I walked in the cooler to find more and when I came out, he pointed the gun at me. I set down the bottle, emptied the register. There was like maybe fifty dollars in there. I handed it to him while he held the gun on me, the tip of it shaking. I was thinking, "Be calm; he won't shoot you," but I remember how stiff my fingers were—and not just from cold. He motioned for me walk into the cooler, and the hardest thing I've ever done is turn my back on that gun.

"Get on your knees."

I paused. I remember lifting my arms just slightly, turning my palms out, drawing air into my chest, chin tipped up, the way a child does when he's about to ask for something. The way my eleven-year-old sister still did, begging gum or other things my mother couldn't afford in the grocery store. In my case, I was trying to ask him not to kill me. If you've never thought, for even a moment, that you were going to die—I mean truly believed it—I will tell you this: Your mind turns first to the most important thing in your life. If you have kids, that's probably what you'd think of. For me, it wasn't my mother or my father or my sisters. It was Aideen.

"Get on your motherfucking knees."

I did it. I kneeled, and I closed my eyes, and I waited in the place I had imagined making love to her. I heard him walk away, and I waited some more. After a while, I cracked open a beer and drank the whole thing, slowly, before I chanced coming out.

They caught him robbing a convenience store three weeks later and asked him what he'd spent the money on. He told them he'd bought clothes for his woman. "They get all crazy on you if you're not careful," is what the police told us he said.

I took a few days off after the robbery. My father didn't say a word, but I knew he thought I'd gotten what I deserved. So there was no question that I'd go back when Mike called, especially when he told me Aideen's parents were back in town. "They'll be watching the kids," he said, which meant Aideen would pretty likely be coming back to work, too. But he didn't say anything about her. He just waited on the line, maybe to see if I'd ask. Maybe also because he felt bad to let her go in right after the place had been robbed. Either way, I didn't take the bait. I told him I'd be in the next day.

That was also the day I got accepted into graduate school at State with a fellowship. I folded the acceptance letter into the back pocket of my jeans, like a ticket. But what I was excited about was seeing Aideen.

It was right before spring break, mid-March. The cold had let up for a couple of weeks but then we'd gotten one of those spring storms, a heavy wet snow. I remember thinking Aideen's parents were probably sorry they'd come up so early, but of course I was glad the weather had held until it was too late for them to change their plans.

Aideen got in an hour or so after I did. It wasn't even dark yet, but I'd been nervous there alone, not wanting any car except hers to slow down and pull in. Watching her walk in, I could almost believe no time had passed at all since that night at Louie's. In fact, I wished we go back to some night before Louie's so that moment would still be ahead of us, and I'd have a chance to do things differently—not better, or right, but in a way that would have made her not want to stop what she'd started.

She surprised me with a hug. "Are you okay?"

I held her until she let go. "Yeah, I'm fine." I didn't want her to know how much the robbery had shaken me. But I wanted her concern. "How about you?" I asked.

The pink band of turtleneck at her throat brought out some color in her face. But up close, her skin seemed too thin, the veins showing through. "We're pretty nervous, you know? Once a place gets hit, word gets around." But then she smiled. She wasn't giving anything away. "We just need to make it through this slump; we'll be fine." She'd almost echoed what Mike had said to me when he'd asked me to work those nights alone. She said it while mixing a 7-Up and vodka—she'd poured out half the 7-Up in the service sink and was filling the bottle back up.

I had a feeling the "we" she was referring to didn't necessarily include the Beer Mart, or Mike, or me, for that matter. I leaned against the spot on the countertop we'd worn smooth with our elbows. "If you think you'll get hit again, how come Mike let you come in at night?"

She took a long swig. I was surprised she could breathe after a gulp like that, but what could I say? I was already on my third beer.

The place made you want to drink. She said, "That's when my mom will watch the kids—when they're sleeping." She shrugged, looked at me for a moment, as if deciding whether to say anything more. "You do what you have to do. You'll see what I mean." She winked at me then, her face flushed, and I knew she still saw me as a kid, not as a man, even after what had happened between us.

My face heated, and I hated that she could see me blushing— further evidence of what she already believed about me. I turned to look at the drive-through, though I knew no one was coming. The conversation seemed to be drifting away from anything I could say to change course. I tried anyway. "You can get out of this," I said.

Maybe she thought I meant the two of them, getting out of the business. Maybe she understood what I'd really meant—it had been a gutless invitation.

"That's what you think," she said, tipping back the bottle again. And that's when I changed my mind about people choosing what happens to them in life. No matter what she said, I couldn't stop wanting her. And what I wanted didn't change a thing.

She leaned against the counter next to me, not so much to be close to me as to get under the heater. We stood with our elbows hooked to the counter behind us, facing the cinder block wall. Beyond that, there was the parking lot and the street leading north, where our lives diverged. I could see that as clearly as if the wall weren't even there.

Jimmy the Brain walked up to the counter so quietly we didn't hear him. "I'd like to get my picture with the Beautiful Aideen," he said. We turned around, startled.

He handed me the camera. "OK," I said, as if he'd actually asked me.

When he stepped back from the counter we both sucked in our breath. He was wearing Jams—those long, flowered shorts—but it wasn't his outfit that shocked me. His legs were papery white and spindly as a doll's. I wanted him to have tougher skin than that, not skin that reminded me of my grandmother.

Aideen came around the counter. "Aren't you cold?" she asked him.

"Not when I'm with you," he said, and she gave him a gracious smile, and I understood exactly how he felt right then. She stood beside him and he hugged her against him and she smiled and said to me, "I'm a trooper!" just as I snapped the picture. I never saw the photo. For all I know there wasn't any film in the camera.

That was the last night I worked with Aideen. When spring break started the following week, Mike had me cover the days, and he did the nights alone. On one of those days, someone came in to buy the neon sign Aideen had ordered back when they'd first opened, which fortunately, in retrospect, only said "BEER MART" instead of the full name Mike had given it upon Aideen's father's sarcastic suggestion. Maybe she'd done it that way to save money, or maybe that was one problem she had foreseen—how to get what they could out of the place if it failed. Or when.

Mike's Beer Mart closed two weeks later. I think Mike was trying to convince Aideen's old man to help them out a little, but it didn't work. The failure must have hit Mike and Aideen hard, because not long after that, Aideen packed up her kids and moved in with her parents. I heard later from my mother that they eventually divorced.

Things had happened just as I'd wanted, back in those months before the winter finally broke. I found a construction job to get me through the summer, and I thought about Aideen every day. But I never got as far as looking up her parents' number.

I saw her in a grocery store a couple years later when I was picking up wine, the kind with a cork and the bottling year printed on the label. I was home for the holidays, my new wife at my parents' house fending off questions from them about when we'd have kids. If Aideen saw me, she didn't show it. Her face was a mask that had begun to pull away from the bones. A few years after that, my mother mentioned hearing that Aideen had gone into rehab. I guess her parents kept the kids.

I've got a kid now. A six-year-old boy. Soft-bellied, red-cheeked, the pads of his feet silky smooth. Still says his "r's" like Jimmy the Brain did. I can't imagine him standing in a warehouse under a jerry-rigged space heater someday, his hair burning and his feet freezing, a gun pointed at his face. No way. I know some people have to work in places like that, and some people choose to do it, like I did, telling myself nobody was going to kill me over a beer, as if my living through that time had been all up to me.

But I still think about Aideen posing for that picture with Jimmy the Brain, shivering maybe not just from cold, clasping her hands together and blowing on them as a polite way to keep her body closed so Jimmy couldn't hug her too close. I want to make sure there's film in the camera. I want to walk with her behind the counter and sit her down under the heater and explain to her how to get out of the business, save her marriage, herself. I want to hold her hands until they're warm again.

What We Do with Loss

D ARREN SAW THE CRASH while at work at the White Sands Villas. After running the sand comber, he was supposed to plant some new palm trees at the front gates; the last ones had died after the hurricane a month before.

It was a clear day, and the air was hot and still. He pulled shovels and fertilizer from the utility closet and then stopped to watch the television in the recreation room, attracted by the bright flower of fire on the screen. Morning sunlight mirrored from the swimming pool outside onto the bottom third of the paneled wall under the TV so that the room seemed to be filling with a watery light. Darren leaned against the pool table, the light warm against his shins, and saw the broken fuselage, the rocky foothills of some western mountain spewing black smoke, the urgent commentary. A plane crash wasn't just a plane crash anymore; the anchors eagerly reminded him. It could be a terrorist attack. Anything. There were no further details but plenty to discuss.

He stepped outside, sand scratching on the smooth brick tiles under his Tevas. Somewhere a siren, then two, began a sweeping whine—likely a heart attack on the beach, a drowning, a drunken driver crashing on the bridge to the Key. Still, he shivered, watching a plane cut a white line across the sky.

Down the rows of stuccoed one-story villas, he watched people emerging from their screened porches and strolling to the beach along the paved pathways: A deeply tanned elderly man wearing peach jogging shorts and sandals. A woman with two children wearing yellow towels around their necks. Two women in bikinis carrying a radio and folding chairs. He couldn't hear what their radio was playing over the slow, steady traffic.

When he came home from work, there was a message on his answering machine from his brother, who typically didn't even call on holidays anymore; they just met up at their parents' house at Christmas and sometimes at Thanksgiving, neutral ground. He listened as his eyes adjusted to the relative dark of his one-bedroom apartment—the chalky gray walls, the shadows of the couch and television.

"You might have seen something on the news," Todd said, his voice calm and businesslike, as if he were scheduling a meeting. "Carrie was on that plane today."

There was a pause, and Darren sat down on a stool at the breakfast bar. Carrie was Todd's wife. "She, she didn't—anyway, she was coming back from a conference and ... that's all I know." Todd left no number, and Darren wondered if he was just distracted with grief, or if he didn't want any calls. There were two more messages, both from his mother, both tearful, asking him to call and assure her that he was okay, even though in Sarasota, he was probably two thousand miles from the crash site.

He arrived in Ohio early the next evening. He'd driven overnight, stopping once at a travel plaza to sleep for a couple of hours. His boss had let him borrow his car; Darren didn't trust his own to make it. He hadn't even considered flying, even if he'd had the money. He pulled into the driveway of his parents' townhouse. There was a small white wreath on the front door and a flag patterned with bright autumn leaves hanging from two plant hooks across the front window. It sagged in the middle, reminding Darren of a man hanging from his wrists. He felt like that as he knocked, the lack of sleep slackening his muscles. He was wearing khakis, a short-sleeved denim shirt, and Tevas, and he felt a chill in the shade. To his left, the trees alongside the street had already lightened to gold and orange at the branch tips.

His mother opened to the door and said his name, and they hugged, and he could smell talcum powder and hairspray. In recent years, each time he saw her, he noticed more silver in her hair, the flesh of her cheeks slightly lower under her wide gray eyes. "You're so brown," she said, which was what she always said, and he couldn't help but smile because this was one detail that made him exotic in a positive way, since a natural tan was impossible to maintain in the long Ohio winters and cloudy, short summers. Other aspects of his life—his decision to drop out of college twenty years ago and his subsequent string of manual jobs—hadn't been as admired. Meanwhile, Todd, four years his junior, had married right after college, MBA and a son by the time he was twenty-five, a vice president's title with an insurance company by the time he was thirty. A nice house in a development near Cuyahoga Falls, two cars, dog, cat. Etcetera.

"You can't avoid the sun down there," Darren said, squeezing his mother tighter before letting her go. She wore a gray wool sweater and black slacks, a decidedly more somber color combination than her usual jewel-toned dresses. He followed her into the kitchen, waited while she poured him a glass of chilled water, listened to the muffled quiet of the house, no television on in the den, no NPR on the radio in the kitchen. Darren had kept the radio on constantly on the drive north, except in parts of West Virginia and southern Ohio where there wasn't good reception. There had been reports on the crash every hour.

Through the sliding glass doors, Darren saw his nephew Shawn on the deck with Todd and his father. The two men stood with their backs to the house, faces tilted upward; on any other day it would seem they were just admiring the colors in the trees. Today Darren couldn't imagine what they might be thinking; his own thoughts were jumpy, unfocused, and every time he closed his eyes he saw only highway. Todd wore a suit; his scalp showed pink-white through the dark thinning hair at his crown. Their father's hair, still thick, was reddish in the late afternoon light, like the wine-colored flannel shirt he wore with khakis. Shawn paced back and forth behind them wearing a baggy long-sleeved shirt and wide-legged, knee-length shorts with high tops. He slumped into a lawn chair and studied his fingers. He would turn fourteen after Christmas.

Watching Shawn, Darren thought of how Todd and Carrie had wanted more children but couldn't have them, and how Carrie, once trim, had over time grown heavier than his plump mother and had taken to wearing more and more makeup and jewelry, as if to distract from the weight gain. These developments had elicited sympathy from his parents, and rightly so, he imagined. But none of his frustrations, at least the ones they knew about, had moved them as much. Once, his mother had called him at his previous job to tell him that Carrie's last round of fertility treatments hadn't taken. His manager had called him into the office and left him alone, as if he, too, expected bad news. *I thought someone had died,* Darren remembered saying; he winced at the memory of it now. *She's just so disappointed,* his mother had said, and Darren was about to ask what she thought he should do—send flowers?—when he realized his mother was really talking about her own disappointment. But even though he wanted to comfort her, he couldn't help but feel that part of the purpose of the call had been to send a message: Where was *his* wife? And children? He considered saying it then: *I'm gay, and the man I love doesn't want to leave his wife, because he's afraid he'll never see his kids again. How's that for disappointed?* It was the closest he'd ever come to a confession. Why that day? He remembered sweating in the air-conditioned maintenance trailer, still breathing hard from unloading boxes. He hadn't said anything because he decided she'd had enough bad news for one day, and that's what telling her would have been—and not just bad news, but also a shock, if his years of careful evasion had worked.

Standing in his parents' kitchen, he tried to picture his mother calling Todd at work just to tell him that Darren had been laid off, or that he was moving again because another landlord had decided to up the rent. He imagined Todd holding his other calls so that he could nod into the phone, and he was about to smile at the ridiculousness of it when his mother handed him the cold glass of water, and then he remembered why he was here; he was here because his sister-in-law had been obliterated in a plane.

"It's so awful," his mother said as if reading the momentary shock in his expression. Her eyes reddened, and she looked away and took a breath and steadied herself. "There were reporters at your brother's house this morning."

"Are they okay?" It was an absurd question, he felt, but he had to ask it. He was trying to prepare himself to open the sliding glass door and walk outside, to shake his brother's hand or maybe hug him—what would be better? They had barely talked for years and it seemed melodramatic to hug him, but then perhaps the situation called for it. Darren needed to decide what to do before they turned around and saw him. But it was Shawn he really ached for. He pictured Shawn the day he was born, dark-haired like Todd, serene and dusky-eyed in his arms, then running around at age five or six. Darren had been in Florida for a couple of years by then and it was hoped but not said that maybe the move was what he needed to find his way; meanwhile, when he came home he could be the fun uncle, and Shawn had loved him with a physical intensity that Darren never saw him show Todd. As a boy, Shawn had thrown himself at Darren's chest, pressed his face into his neck. Remembering this, it was Shawn he wanted to hug. At least that was a real emotion, something to start with.

But if he was being real, then he also had to admit to himself that he didn't believe he would miss Carrie—her materialistic, status-conscious personality, leasing cars so she could always have the latest model, buying so many gifts at Christmas for Shawn that the wrappings filled several large trash bags; it seemed an apology for her constant traveling. She had asked Darren last Thanksgiving, "Don't you think it's time to buy a house?" As if that would resolve whatever shortcomings she'd seen in him. If he were a jerk for thinking these things about her at a time like this, then so be it.

His mother was talking, had been talking for several minutes, about how Todd wanted to go to the crash site but hadn't wanted to take Shawn, and anyway Carrie's parents were already there; they were staying in a hotel and trying to figure out what to do. There were no plans yet for a funeral; Todd was thinking about leaving the next day and Shawn would stay with them over the weekend.

"I better go outside and say hello," Darren said.

"Yes, let's—well, I'll be out there in a minute," his mother said.

He checked to make sure the door wasn't locked before trying to open it; he was conscious of trying to look confident, smooth in his movements. He always felt this sense of theater whenever he came to visit, because he knew he wasn't being entirely himself. Maybe, he thought as he pulled the door open and met their turning faces with a close-lipped smile that he hoped showed both happiness for being there and a sense of sadness for what had happened, it was because he wondered what they knew about him and never said in his presence. But what could they have discerned from their few visits, staying at hotels along Midnight Pass Road on the Key since he'd always rented apartments that were too small for guests, keeping them bare as possible so as not to reveal whatever relationship he was in at the time?

"Todd," he heard himself saying. They shook hands, then hugged. Now the situation felt real; he could feel his brother's heartbeat, could smell his shaving lotion and toothpaste, and he tried to remember when he'd last hugged him. He turned next to Shawn and hugged him, Shawn turning his face away, an arm loose around Darren's shoulders, not wanting to be hugged maybe, not wanting to be anywhere. Then he shook hands with his father, whose narrow face was stern with grief.

"Glad you're here," Darren's father said.

"Glad to be here," Darren said automatically. But thought, *Where else would I be?* This was how his father dismantled him, thanking him for doing things anyone would consider appropriate, as if he hadn't quite expected Darren to come through, and his response had sounded hollow and stupid. He slid his hands into his pockets. Shawn turned his back to all of them, cracking his knuckles. Darren remembered he had left his glass of water inside. "Can I bring anyone anything?"

"I'm fine," his father said.

Todd shook his head, and Shawn said nothing. Darren found his glass of water on the table next to the sliding glass door; he didn't remember setting it there in his anxiety about making sure he didn't fumble his entrance. He could hear his mother moving around upstairs. He'd meant to go right back outside, but the idea of it made him nervous. Instead he climbed the stairs and walked down the hallway to his parents' bedroom. "Can I help with anything?" he asked through the half-open door.

"No. I'm going to pick up some dinner in a little bit, so there's nothing to do," she called from the bathroom. "Just make yourself comfortable."

He walked back down the hallway, down the stairs, looked at the purpling sky from the breakfast room. *Make yourself comfortable.* He longed to be comfortable, here of all places, to forget himself and give in to the reality that had come to his family, his sister-in-law dead. He wanted to feel grief, to cry, to be angry at least. On one radio show he'd listened to coming through Akron, reporters talked about a local fireman, father of four, who had died with his wife and two older children on the plane on the way to accept a national service award. It was easier to feel sorry for that man's family than his own brother, maybe because he didn't know them and his sympathy wasn't complicated by a resentment he knew he shouldn't feel. If this made him sick and self-absorbed, then so be it. Better to be truthful, at least to himself, about what he was thinking. He opened the sliding glass door, water in hand, just as his father turned to come in. He stepped aside to let everyone pass.

"Getting cool out," his father said.

Todd sat on one end of the couch. His cell phone rang; he checked the incoming call number, and put it back in his pocket. "The office," he said with a tight smile to Darren, who sat across from him.

"Nothing that can't wait, probably," Darren said. It was unusual for Todd to ignore a call, no matter from where or when it came; at last year's Thanksgiving, for example, he'd talked right at the table, with Carrie rolling her eyes and smiling apologetically at Darren's parents, but clearly she'd found it amusing; it was part of their shared persona, Carrie and Todd, the high-powered, deal-making professionals.

"I'm going to check on dinner," their father said, heading upstairs. Shawn leaned on the piano, tracing an invisible design in its finish.

"Come sit," Todd said. An order, not an invitation. Shawn sat in the chair next to Darren.

"Well, so you're staying here this weekend?" Darren asked Shawn. He had no idea what to say to Todd; it was difficult to talk with him even in the best of times, even when he'd been in love and happy with the life he'd chosen, the warm secret of his simple existence, a non-pretentious job, a person he chose to be with, rather than held together by the weight of possessions and position the way he imagined Todd and Carrie were. He didn't know when he'd lost the ability to talk to his brother; perhaps after Todd had married, not immediately, but gradually, as their lives had filled with new responsibilities, or as Todd's had.

"Probably," Shawn said. He sounded defeated. "I don't know."

"Yes, you're going to stay here, like we discussed," Todd said, his voice tight in his throat, impatient. It was perhaps a cliché to think how grief aged one, but to Darren he seemed suddenly much older, slouched on the sofa, hands clasped tight under his belly. Darren wondered if he would even recognize Todd if he saw him somewhere unexpected.

Their mother came downstairs, followed by their father. "Chinese, okay?" she said.

"I'll get it," Darren said, standing. Before anyone could object or offer him money, he turned to Shawn. "Want to come?" He didn't look at Todd to see if he found this invitation acceptable. Shawn nodded and followed him to the door.

"Where to?" Darren asked him outside. His unfamiliarity with the town after so many years was more comforting than he'd expected.

"I'll show you," Shawn said.

Darren shut off the radio as soon as he started the car, in case the news was on. He moved so fast to push the power button that Shawn looked at him, questioning. Darren pretended not to notice.

"I'm not sure what else to do except to ask you, Shawn," he said as they drove toward town. "Are you okay?"

Shawn shook his head slowly, looking out the window. "I don't know. I can't feel anything. I can't think."

Darren thought of saying that at some point it would hit him, and then it would be hard, but he stopped himself. "I guess probably everyone's saying this to you, but I'm here for you whenever you want to talk. Or if you want to get away, you know? You could come down for a while and stay. I could teach you to sail."

Shawn seemed not to have heard him. Then, after a moment, "I can't. I've got school."

"Surely they're not—" Darren stopped himself again. "Well." He waited. "I want you to know you're one of my favorite people in the world. I mean it. I've loved you your whole life, and we will get through this." He thought he might cry for a moment, not from sadness but from the relief of saying something he meant, from speaking openly.

Shawn nodded, still not looking at him. "Thanks."

Darren thought about thirteen. His sexuality had emerged for him slowly; in his late teens and early twenties he'd tried sex with more than a few women, a test to see if he'd been right. But that first twinge of the other had arrived at the age Shawn was now; yes, he remembered walking around perpetually between tears and a fistfight, masturbating quickly in the one stall in the boy's bathroom at school, trembling afterward sometimes for hours from the force of his orgasm. He remembered thirteen as the year he'd started to fear he might rip open with so much anger and desire and so little of his known self to steady him.

He wanted to tell Shawn that he understood not just the age, but also the loss. He could hear himself saying the words: *My first lover died of AIDS. Not my first relationship, but the first person I loved. He was infected before I knew him. Neither of us intended to get involved; we were friends. He knew he would die. He was still married and living with his wife. He had two small children and sometimes we took them to the water park or to movies. We'd both tried and failed with women, and now we knew who we were, and we just wanted to enjoy our time quietly. But I fell in love with him. I wanted him to leave his family. Now I regret that I asked him to make that choice. When he died I took the day off to go to his funeral, and then I just went on.*

Darren knew that to tell Shawn these things now was selfish, born more of the desire to show his own credentials with grief than to respect his nephew's. He watched the boy swing his legs out of the car in the parking lot, a sleepwalker. It exhausts you, he wanted to say, but he kept that to himself, too.

Shawn picked out everyone's meals, including Darren's, and they drove back to the house. The neon and florescent lights of the take-out counter seemed to enliven him. On the way back, he talked about starting high school next year, and how he'd heard the seniors would stuff you in a closet or a locker if you weren't careful.

Darren laughed. "So they're still saying that."

"Yeah," Shawn said. He had his father's coloring, but just then, maybe with the light nearly gone, he looked very much like Carrie, too—her nose, her chin, the arch of her eyebrows all accentuated by the streetlights flicking on as they passed. Driving at night often made Darren think of being on the water, the tire-whisper like a wind-ruffled sail, the traffic lights distant blinking buoys. "Do you remember visiting that time?"

"Yeah. I was, like, four. You had a huge boat and we went fishing."

The boat Shawn was talking about was a general charter, and there were other passengers on board, but Darren didn't correct him. Carrie and Todd were starting out then, Todd still driving the Nova their father had bought used for him, Shawn's bed in the dining nook of a one-bedroom apartment. Darren had just moved to Florida, and Todd had taken the family to visit him, and that was the last time he remembered feeling totally comfortable with his brother, showing him around, impressing him with his newly discovered talent for sailing. But that day on the boat, a man Darren knew casually, an older man who had shown interest in him, was a passenger, too. Darren saw him coming and had tried to signal him to stop, a subtle shake-off, but he'd kept coming, and there was no doubt what he was, in his orange silk tank top, white pajama pants and woven leather slippers, a diamond in each ear, his cologne heavy in the hot air. Darren had had no choice but to introduce him to Carrie and Todd and even Shawn, whom Carrie pulled against her legs. And worse, the older man had brushed Darren's upper arm with his fingertips and mouthed *Call me* before walking away. Darren wondered if Carrie and Todd had ever told their parents. He remembered Todd's discomfort, maybe not so much with the man's presence, as with Darren's exposure; it was embarrassing to him. And Carrie's reaction, though it had disgusted him at the time, seemed tragic and forgivable to him now, how she'd wanted to protect her son, that simple mother's love.

They'd never spoken of it. After that, there was never another visit except from his parents, and every time he came north the time he spent alone with his brother grew shorter and shorter, until their conversations took place only in the company of family. One time it had pleased him to see the irritation on his brother's face when Shawn insisted on sitting in Darren's lap, kissing his ear with loud smacks and hanging from his neck, too young to be aware that these actions weren't masculine, and that his uncle was maybe not dangerous but certainly not safe. Not *normal*.

Shawn carried the bags and Darren held the door for him. His mother laid everything out on the table; his father asked if anyone wanted a beer.

"I'll have one," Shawn said, and Darren's mother laughed, almost too loud, as if grateful for the excuse.

"You'll have to wait, young man."

The men had beers; Darren's mother poured herself a glass of white Zinfandel. They sat down, and Todd began eating his food steadily and slowly, and everyone else followed suit. Darren was again conscious of the lack of television or radio; usually at least one was playing during family dinners. He realized he had very little appetite once he started eating, so he took his time. He stole glances at his father's and mother's faces, realizing that they too were trying and failing to think of something to say, as paralyzed as he; finally, he gave in to the silence.

After dinner, he followed his brother out to the deck with two fresh beers. When he offered Todd one, he shook his head. "No, I'm fine."

"Take it," Darren said. The command in his tone surprised him. Todd took the beer. They stood and sipped for a few moments. The air was cold now, thin. Darren thought of the watery warm light of the recreation room where he'd watched footage of the burning plane, the moment he'd heard his brother's even voice on the answering machine, the way their bodies moved through the air, tender and fragile. "What can I do? To help you," he asked. Todd had once looked to him for guidance on everything from how to throw a ball to how to ask women out, a memory that made him smile. And there'd been that one night when they were much younger—Todd was about six or seven and still wetting the bed at night. He was supposed to get up and tell their mother and then help change the sheets; the family doctor had said this would help break the habit. One night, Darren woke to Todd crying quietly. He knew what had happened, and he threw back the covers of his twin bed and whispered to him to get in. Todd pulled off his wet pajama bottoms and got in next to Darren, naked from the waist down. He rolled onto his side with his back to Darren. Darren scooted back against the wall to give Todd room, but Todd had pressed back against him, wanting to be held. Darren could feel the damp of his brother's buttocks against his belly where his own pajama top had ridden up, and he could smell the urine, but he made himself put an arm across Todd's chest to comfort him. He hugged him close until his breathing calmed and he fell asleep. Did Todd remember that too? Did he ever wonder if Darren had been motivated by anything other than love, even then?

"I don't know," Todd was saying. "Right now, we just have to see how things go. I have to talk with Carrie's parents, with the airline, with our lawyer. It's just—" he stopped, sipped his beer, shook his head. He was fighting tears; his voice clamped down in his throat. Darren stepped toward him, but Todd stiffened, so he stopped. "There's too much," Todd mumbled then, staring at the dark trees beyond the deck. He seemed to have contained himself again.

Darren wanted to say he understood: There was too much, and never enough. He wanted to tell him how much he loved Shawn, and how he believed the best of Carrie would live in him, but he knew these were the words people used when there was nothing else to be done. They were a visitor's way of saying good-bye before going back to a life that still fit together. This was what we did with loss, Darren thought, when we saw it in others or when it blew open our own lives; we tried to contain it with small gestures so it wouldn't overwhelm us. At his lover's funeral, Darren had watched this repeat performance in the procession greeting his lover's wife and family: the clasping of hands, the hugging, the murmured condolences. At the time, he was glad to have been spared it; now, he believed the only alternative was his presence in that procession, as true as he could make it.

A movement in the living room caught his attention; he turned to see his mother snapping open a white tablecloth over the dining room table, centering it as it drifted down over the dark wood. Darren thought she was doing what she could do, smoothing the cloth under her palms. He touched his brother's shoulder.

"Look," he said, nodding toward their mother, who was now setting a vase of flowers on the table. She straightened and turned to the glass.

"We're here," Darren said, although he wasn't sure she could hear him. Then he led his brother inside.

Monks

My wife had left me and I was looking for a place. Couldn't make the house payments installing cable and she didn't want it so I had to sell and split the difference. She still had the telemarketing job here in Red Stick, I knew from trying her complaint line from a payphone in the Thirsty Tiger—and I did have complaints, none of which were covered under warranty. But it was just a matter of time and she'd be gone. Maybe to her parents in Missouri City, maybe down to Galveston, where she always said she'd move if she could figure out how to make a living there. "Don't even call me," she'd said. And I hadn't, except that once.

"So you're the cable guy, huh?" Jem said, and I nodded. We sat on the front porch of a rental house off I-10. Squat narrow houses, tight as teeth, with dirt strip yards and broken pavement. Two doors down, a couple of teenaged girls squealed as three guys, standing on their bike pedals, skimmed close enough to brush the girls' bare shoulders with their outstretched hands. The girls hugged their haltered breasts, giggled, hips slung toward the boys as if dragged in their wake.

I took a hit from my can of beer. Bud. Shit beer, thirty or forty of them in the bottom of the fridge Jem had pointed to when I came in. "Help yourself," he'd said. Nothing else except a bottle of orange juice and a tub of Velveeta.

Jem wasn't the owner; that was Bruchemme, who was on his

way home from his repo job at Mullis. Jem said he went by Brue. I was waiting for Brue to show so I could work out the details. I'd called on the newspaper ad earlier that day and Jem said he'd be there to show me the place. Brown carpeted living room with two couches and a rug, stereo on the floor. Big bare kitchen with stained cabinets standing open. Tried to close one and it popped back again. Jem and Brue had the two second-floor bedrooms. I looked at the attic room, a ten-by-ten box in the crotch of the roof, one small window, barely enough to put a bed in, two hundred a month. Part of me thought this was just what I needed, an empty room, a way to strip myself clean. Part of me wanted to beg no one in particular to give me my life back. I wanted the flowered wallpaper in the kitchen, my wife's slips cool and folded in the drawers.

"So, Vincent. Could you hook us up with some free cable?" Jem was asking.

"Could you hook me up with some free rent when I lose my job?" I said. Jem laughed and I managed a smile. People asked me stuff like that all the time; I was prepared.

A hot breeze crossed the porch. Down the street, trucks rattled on the overpass, their red runner lights streaking like dying stars against the orange-brown sky. No moon; just heat, the porch chairs tacky with it.

One of the teenage girls down the street yelped. Jem grunted. "Like to have a little of that."

I nodded, because that's what you do when you're drinking a beer with a guy you don't know and he starts talking about women—girls—like they're on the menu. You go with it and you feel a step closer to the old men sitting in the back row for the short flicks, the bags around their bottles gone soft. You can be a family man, a player or a felon. A few men can switch from one to the other; most get going one way and can't turn around. Jem was about twenty-five. He thought he'd have time to figure it out. I was thirty-five and thought I'd already nailed it. But now I was back at the beginning and I didn't want to be here.

"You shoot stick?" Jem asked.

"Sure."

"Ever go down to Slippy's?"

I knew the place, but I hadn't been in years. I shook my head.

"Well, if you end up here, you should come out with us. Brue and I can clean the joint. Drink free all night." Jem lit a cigarette, words pressed between his teeth.

"I'm not that good," I said.

"You'll get better after a while. Hey, you could help us shark."

I shrugged a maybe. He was a big-shouldered guy with soft features and a small nose. Ball cap backwards on his head. Out of college a couple of years. He'd told me he was working with some kind of dot com, and he'd pointed to his white Lexus with the tinted windows, either to explain the reason or the result. Of course, that gig busted within the year, but right then he had money, a lot of it.

He blew out smoke, and as it thinned above us he checked his cell phone, frowned. He was already tired of me, I figured. He felt sorry for me. He was pretty sure he wouldn't be living in some attic room when he was my age.

"You need a cell phone or you pay for a line. Brue and I got cells."

"That's fine," I said. I wasn't expecting any calls.

"So you'll have to come out and play sometime. I mean, Slippy's is a funny place. Some nights we can't lose, and some nights guys'll come in and we can't stay on the table ten minutes. The lady that owns the place, little Thai lady, she beats the shit outta anybody. Phenomenal."

"What do you bet?" I asked.

"Drinks, pretty much. Maybe ten bucks a rack or so, but I ain't in it for the money, see." He slipped his cell in his back pocket, rested his elbows on his knees, and opened his hands, the way a guy does when he's going to give you some wisdom. "It's just a beautiful game, you know? Last Friday Brue sank the eight ball on the best shot I've ever seen, a two-bank in the far corner. Had to be perfect to make it. And you know what the two chach's playing us said? 'You didn't call the banks, man!'" He slurred his words and dropped his voice to imitate them. "And let me tell you, there was only one way you could make that shot. But those guys had to get technical because they don't want to lose. Don't get me wrong, man, we don't like to lose either. But that's part of life, right? You gotta lose sometime."

A Jeep pulled up, some kind of rap pounding on the stereo. "That's Brue," Jem said.

I couldn't see him until he stepped under the porch light, grinning with an unlit cigarette clamped between his teeth. He stopped to light it and, squinting through the smoke, put a hand out to shake with me. I leaned forward to meet it, and he said, "Don't get up, now," even though I wasn't trying to. "You need a beer?"

I lifted mine to show I had one.

"Fine, I'll be right back," he said. He came back with a beer and a bong—a piece of clear PVC tube with a hole drilled for the pipe. He packed it and offered it to me. "No man, thanks," I said.

"You don't mind if I partake, though, do you?" He was well-spoken, hitting all the consonants.

"No, go ahead."

He smoked up the bowl, repacked it, and passed it to Jem, who started in on it. He sat back on the porch railing and his legs dangled. He was small—I thought he would be big because of the repo job and everything Jem told me about what he'd done to the house as he'd showed me around, like hanging sheet rock in the attic. "He can turn a piece of shit into gold, that guy," Jem had said, pulling the string to cut off the bare lightbulb hanging from the ceiling.

Brue dragged on his cigarette and inhaled deeply, turning to smile at me before he let go of the smoke. His teeth were small and pointed, and he had red lips and quick dark eyes. "So, Jem showed you around?"

"I told you I would," Jem said before I could answer. He sounded like a kid saying he'd done his chores.

"He did," I said.

"You like it?"

"Yeah, sure. It's fine."

"I gotta fix the toilet behind the kitchen. And the dryer's out in the basement and I gotta find the right parts for that, too. But she's a good place," he said, slapping the porch railing. He finished his cigarette and started a new one. He offered the pack to me and then to Jem. I waved them off.

"I got my own," Jem said.

Brue looked surprised. "Hell just got a little colder today," he said.

Jem wrapped his arms around himself and shivered. "Satan's like, 'I'm damn freezing!'"

Brue laughed, indulgent. He had a full deep voice that seemed too big for him and an exaggerated politeness, or generosity, as if he owned everything and was just lending it to you out of the goodness of his heart. He looked to be about the same age as Jem, but those spare features and flushed cheeks made him seem too healthy, like he was draining the life out of everything around him.

Jem said, "Hey, I was telling him about that eight ball shot the other night, and those chach's bitching about it."

"Yeah, they were pissed," Brue said, flicking his cigarette at the ground behind him. "But that shot was so beautiful I knew it couldn't get any better, so I said I might as well go home."

"You gave up the table?" I asked.

"You gotta play by the rules," Brue said in a patient tone.

"Even if they're chach's with their gold chains and Camaros," Jem said.

"Even then," Brue said with a fatherly smile. He got up, offered beers, and I took another one. He packed and smoked another bowl, and Jem did the same. I passed again, but I breathed in the hot sweet smoke they blew out and let myself think about her, the way she tied a wrap skirt across the rounded bones of her hips, the lift of her breasts as she pulled on a camisole.

"So, what brings you here?" Brue asked me.

"Just looking for a new place," I said. "I need something for a few months." Which wasn't exactly true. I didn't even know where I'd be in a month. I didn't want to be alive. But there was the fact of me, heavy in my chair, listening to Jem start in about a guy named Dorf who couldn't play a quarter table but could run the Cadillacs every time. "One time," Jem said, "I was at a party over at Dorf's place, and he and his girlfriend were doing the deed, and when he was through, he came out naked and jumped on me. Can you believe that?"

"Disgusting human being," Brue said, shaking his head.

"I wasn't right for a couple of weeks after that," Jem said. "Felt like Luke Skywalker when he got dragged into the ice cave by that mammoth thing."

"Wonder whatever happened to him?" Brue said. And we all waited, as if one of us was going to come up with the answer somehow. He got up again. "OK, last beer for me before I turn in. Anybody else?"

We both said no. Jem asked me what I thought of Brue, and I said he seemed fine to me. Then he said, "Brue knows how to take an opportunity. He's got five houses he's fixing up, and he's only twenty-six."

"Pretty good," I said.

"He takes what comes to him. I mean, even," Jem dropped his head and laughed. "Even women. I dumped this girl once and she went that same day to see Brue and he took her on. Brue's like, 'Are you pissed, man?' and I said no, but I mean, what if she hadn't taken a shower in between? I mean, that's sick. But that's Brue for you."

"Shit," I said, because I couldn't think of anything else.

"Totally."

Brue came back, and Jem's cell phone rang, and after he checked the number on the display he got up to head inside. "Hey, baby," he said as he shut the door behind him.

"Booty call," Brue said, winking. Then, "Come on, what's your story?"

I didn't say anything. Brue leaned forward. "I see a lot of people come and go in my work. You still got a groove on your finger, man."

"Like I said, I'm just passing through." I was hot, this kid pushing me. I wanted to choke him, and he could read it. He leaned back again, looked down the street, where the girls were still chattering on the sidewalk. They grabbed each other's hands and gestured wildly, aping what they saw in the movies, maybe, except when movie heroines talked, someone actually wanted to hear it. Brue snorted as if to say they weren't worth his notice, and busied himself lighting another cigarette. I wanted to go to them and take their waving arms, walk them inside. I wanted to warn them about loss. But I didn't really know anything about that yet. In a year I'd find out my wife had left me with a baby two months grown in her belly, and then I'd spend the next year going to court proving I was good enough to see my daughter. In a few more years, I'd stop blaming myself for not being the man my wife thought she'd met at the air show when I'd flown Cessnas with the Sky Kings. The man I actually was went from one job to the next, and then sold the plane to buy a house while the credit cards got thicker with debt. It's true that I didn't feel I added up to much, sitting on that porch. But I would find out that I could watch my daughter grow up in once-a-month visits, all the time betting she'd want to see me again. That I could stick it out, that it would be enough.

"My parents split when I was seven," Brue said. "It's a bitch." He took a drink from his beer, tipping his head way back. Jem came out again.

"Any luck?" Brue asked.

Jem shook his head, grinning.

"No poontang fo' you!" Brue whooped. He stretched out and balanced himself on the railing. He crossed his legs at the ankles, balancing them, too, beer in one hand, cigarette in the other. "I was in the Home Depot yesterday, looking for those dryer parts, which they didn't have—I forgot about the toilet being screwed up too—and I'm walking around, pissed at being there on my day off, anyway, you know, and I was passing the tools section, and there's these three Buddhist monks looking at drills. They're in the full nine yards, orange robes and shaved heads, and they were all excited about these tools. Passing them around and jabbering. And I thought, what's wrong with me, when they're having such a good goddamn time?" He tilted his head back to look into the eaves.

"Fucking profound," Jem said.

"Sure," I said. I thought about sleeping in that hot box under the roof. I thought about my wife driving away. Down the street, the girls in the halter tops turned and walked into a house, arms crossed, voices lilting, disappointed. The yellow light bulb on their porch went dark. I knew I was at the beginning of something I had to survive. I stood up, reached for my wallet, and counted out my cash.

Lowell's Lines

B ECAUSE I PREDICTED my father's death, my Aunt Lowell says I already know more than my mother, who is taking summer classes at the community college where my father taught surveying. Aunt Lowell, also a teacher like her brother—high school physics, retired—was named after Percival Lowell, the then-famous author of *Mars as the Abode of Life,* published in 1908, in which he theorized that Mars' canals were built by intelligent beings. My father, born four years later, got Percival, but always went by Pull. The fact that Lowell was wrong about the canals is beside the point, Aunt Lowell will tell you. The point is he had ideas.

Aunt Lowell says my mother has already moved on, if a recent meeting I happened upon between her and a certain young man at the library adds up to anything other than "cramming"—as my mother puts it—for algebra tests. Aunt Lowell says women can know things in the absence of evidence; there is a reason the Scientific Method was invented by a man, and it's not because they were ever smarter. For example, when she finds me frowning in front of the oval mirror which hung in my parents' lake cottage until my mother and I moved in with Aunt Lowell three months ago, she knows what I'm thinking without even looking straight at me. She says, "Beauty isn't achieved by what you hide, but what you draw the eye to."

I'm trying to find something to wear which doesn't make me look like I've hung flour bags around my hips. I've tugged on my low rider jeans with flowers up the seams (no chance), a pair of wide-legged pleated shorts that my mother was actually getting rid of because they are out of style but can at least be buttoned (dowdy), and a long black knit skirt and sweater set, which are too heavy for the weather but seem to be doing the trick when I stand with my stomach sucked in and hip cocked and one foot turned out just slightly, like a JC Penney's model. This is the skirt I wore to Pull's funeral, with a white blouse so that I looked like a waiter, and I'm wondering if enough time has passed to wear it to Dairy Queen on a date with my boyfriend Bartlett Fetter, whose taste in food is just one of the many personal qualities that failed to impress my father. "Think about 'Fetter,'" Pull said to me not long before he died, crossing his wrists behind his back like a handcuffed prisoner. A *decent interval*, that's what I'm wondering about.

"Hmm?" I say. I heard what Aunt Lowell said, but the meaning flickers and misses me.

Aunt Lowell puts her pink hands on her soft, wide hips. She looks like she could teach you more about muffins than subatomic particles, but she says that's the problem with looking—you miss too much. She narrows her eyes the way she probably did to former students caught not paying attention—and the way she does with me when she tells me I am the one who should be in college, not my mother. Speaking slowly, she repeats herself: "Beauty isn't achieved by what you hide, but what you draw the eye to."

My mother hears this as she comes in and drops her red satchel on the counter. I can see a groove in her bare shoulder from the straps. She's wearing low-slung jeans and a stretchy blue camisole, the kind of thing she used to wear under a blouse tied at the waist with lined slacks. Sunglasses perched on her head, she looks like any other college student, at least from what I can tell from watching the clientele at Suds & Duds, where I fold laundry for two dollars and twenty-five cents an hour.

"You don't end sentences with prepositions, Lowell," my mother says, a glitter of victory in her eyes from showing off what she knows. In that way, she's more like Aunt Lowell than she'd like to admit, but then Aunt Lowell would say that what my mother knows is not a lot.

Aunt Lowell and my mother regard each other in the narrow space between the oven and the refrigerator. My mother's ponytail is folded with the ends tucked into the rubber band the way girls are doing today—my hair is too thin to do this and anyway I have just cut it short—and she leans against the counter to show she'd be comfortable in this stand-off for as long as might be required.

Aunt Lowell smiles, dipping her chin, and I think for a moment she's giving over the point. But she says, "Did you hear about the farm boy who got into Harvard and asked 'Where's the bathroom at?' The professor said, 'We don't end our sentences with prepositions.' So the farm boy says,"—and she does a fair drawl here—"'All right, where's the bathroom at, asshole?'"

My mother sucks in her breath, and Aunt Lowell giggles, pleased with herself, and then my mother picks up her satchel, rolling her eyes, and heads for the bedroom she and I officially share, though in practice I sleep on the couch because she snores. Aunt Lowell turns back to me. She told me once that after she retired, she lived in fear for an entire year that she would die, because she'd never married and work had been her life. Some days she was too scared to drive to the grocery store. "Just like a man, cowering," she'd said. But when she hadn't died, she realized she was free. "Are you going out with that drip?" she asks me now. Surviving her freedom has made her honest.

This question is a variation on a theme. I recently made up a cheeky stock answer but now I can't remember it. Usually, I have a great memory. For example, the mention of Harvard made me think of how Percival Lowell's younger brother Abbott was president of Harvard and his sister Amy was a poet.

"He's not a drip," I say, fighting a yawn, not only because I'm sleepy but because the effort of defending him makes me tired. In fact, no matter how much I sleep, exhaustion envelops me like gauze.

"You're happy with a paddleboat enthusiast?" Aunt Lowell says.

Before I can stop myself, I roll my eyes, just like my mother did. I can hear her washing her face in the bathroom, three quick splashes over the pedestal sink. When I go into the guest room to put on lipstick and comb my hair, I will find her stretched belly-down on the blue bedspread, ankles crossed, chin cupped in her hands, fingertips resting lightly on her freshly-washed cheeks, reading one of her textbooks, or, really, assuming the position of one who reads serious material because she must. She will not look up. She will be a woman who is doing something worthwhile, beautifully. I've heard grief ages you, but she seems to have shed ten years since Pull drowned.

I turn away from Aunt Lowell, hoping she didn't see my reaction. I've decided it won't help to mention, as I have in the past, that Bartlett has built his own telescope, just like Percival Lowell, though his is not as large, and that he is credited with discovering an actual star. I look in the mirror and conclude that it's okay to wear the skirt, because it's not the kind of thing my father would've cared about. It's a useless consideration, how long you wait to wear something after a funeral, even your father's funeral, where the room smelled like lake and the eulogy faded into the moss green walls. My father cared that I got a good education and that I said thank you to people. He cared that I was his only child and that I would be loved. "His name is Bartlett," I say to Aunt Lowell. "He maintains paddleboats. It's a family business."

Aunt Lowell looks at me as if surprised I believe what I'm saying. It's not because any of the information isn't true; it's because I think it counts for something in my life. This is where she disagrees. She looks at me as if she's already seen this play out and she's just waiting for me to catch up. She hasn't made any comments about my clothes fitting tighter; maybe she doesn't want to make me feel any worse when she's already ridiculing my boyfriend. I doubt it's because she hasn't noticed. But I also doubt she's guessed it's because I'm pregnant. Because if she did have even an inkling, I'd be able to read it in her eyes as clearly as her namesake saw canals etched on a desert planet.

BARTLETT FETTER'S FATHER collects autographed celebrity headshots, which he hangs on the paneled walls. He used to display his favorite, Rock Hudson, in a frame next to the register on the rental counter until he found out The Rock was gay. Bartlett Fetter used to have a younger brother until Fetter Senior found out he was gay, too. Bartlett thinks Paton, who dropped out of high school and ran away, is winning big money in drag queen competitions in Asheville. Paton is a family name, but Bartlett thinks being named Paton and seeing the Rock Hudson photo every day may have contributed to his orientation. I've wondered if Bartlett has any concerns for himself because his name is unusual and he saw that same photo too, every summer, working for his father, who berates him constantly. Bartlett just takes it. Some people might think this is weak, but I think it shows a certain kind of grace, refusing to fight back. Truthfully, I'm not worried about his sexual orientation because he wants to have sex all the time.

I wait for Bartlett in the gravel lot beside Aunt Lowell's apartment building in order to spare him her "failing student" look—lips pressed together in resigned sympathy. I lean against her pollen-dusted green Ford and gaze at the narrow alley between her bedroom window and the garage, which the owner uses for storage now. The two gardenia bushes she planted when she moved in have fattened so that you can barely squeeze by them to sit in the small iron chairs she wedged in there. Holding a curling lattice against the garage wall is a table she made from a birdbath topped with a piece of pathway slate. Honeysuckle fingers the gutter. Once it gets dark, Aunt Lowell will turn on the white string lights she wove through the lattice and sit in one of her tiny chairs, sipping from a glass of Red Zinger iced-tea until I come home. My mother will be asleep.

Bartlett picks me up in his silver blue Chevy Caprice, one of those wide-bodied police models. It was his father's before. On

Fridays, like today, it gleams with wax and I find vacuum tracks on the velour seats. But they are grease-stained from when his father carried paddleboat parts to the marina for repair, and the moldy smell of dried lakewater rises under the citrus-scented cleanser Bartlett rubs into the dash with a strip of undershirt. I like that he takes care of things, even worn out, rattling things; it seems hopeful. He leans to kiss me when I get in. "You look nice," he says, which is what he always says, and that seems hopeful, too.

"I think I'm in the mood for fish," I tell Bartlett.

He nods slowly and drives down the hill, and I know he's thinking about when he suggested fish about a month ago, and I started crying. Then, it was because I was nauseous and had just figured out it wasn't the flu or grief but pregnancy, and on top of that I was still in a full-on war with water. I had decided to give up swimming or eating anything that lived in it. And this was a lot to promise, because I grew up swimming and eating fish, two of my father's favorite things to do. Also, if you're honest with yourself, which I try to be, you have to admit bathing kind of breaks the boycott, and the truth is everything comes from water; it's the basis of life. That's why Lowell was looking so hard for it in the observatory he built in Flagstaff. Eventually, he found the canals were easier to see if he partially covered the lens. When he died in 1916, he didn't know his canals were a trick of the imagination, and this, I think, was a blessing.

When Bartlett pulls into the parking lot of The Crab Shack, he turns to me, eyebrows raised, long face framing a careful smile, fully expecting me to change my mind. I open my car door and as I get out I tell myself that Pull would have been happy that I've given up my war on water, and he would have been happier still about a grandchild, even though I'm nineteen, and even though it is Bartlett Fetter's.

We sit at a two-top next to a huge fish tank with blue and yellow angels flickering like winked eyelids in the lit water. My elbows stick to the table. Bartlett's eyebrows seem to meet at the slight ridge of bone above his nose, shadowed in blue because of the tank, a feature my father had once pointed to as evidence the Fetters were not as evolved as the rest of us.

"Are you going to get a beer or anything?" I ask him when the waitress comes.

He orders two drafts, but I shake my head. "I'll just have water," I tell her.

Bartlett smiles, hazel eyes narrowed just slightly in question—yes, I'd sworn off drinking water, too, just the pure form, of course, but again, you have to be honest about what's in juice or iced tea. Bartlett had listened to me rage about water for hours. There was nothing else to blame. He was the one who held my hair back from my face when I threw up after the funeral, kneeling in the gravel parking lot, with Fetter Senior nearby, barking about how death can upset the stomach. Bartlett would be considered handsome if his chin didn't go on as long as it did. I think of our baby with that chin, that ridge of forehead. "Bartlett," I say, "I'm pregnant."

Bartlett reaches for his paper-rolled silverware at the top of his plate with both hands, like a lever he might pull. He leans on his elbows, tips his forehead close to me. "What?" he says.

"I'm due in February."

Bartlett closes his eyes and shakes his head as if dizzy from standing up too quickly. He used to get terrible nosebleeds in school in the winter—the dry air from the rattling wall heaters set him off—and I remember wondering if the loss of blood ever made him lightheaded. It seemed to be so much, seeping between his fingers as he jumped from his desk in American Government and made for the hallway. He was retaking the class my junior year. I'd known him for years from the lake, but the fact that he was a year older made him a shadowy figure for me until then. In summer I wore only a tank suit and tennis shoes and fished off the dock with my father. Bartlett was often only a few feet away, wearing cutoffs and no shirt, holding the paddleboats steady for mothers and kids to board. We were nearly naked for months at a time, but we'd never so much as said each other's names. It took being in class together for us to become real to each other. He'd failed so many classes he'd had to repeat his junior year, and after a few months I put it together (because Bartlett isn't dumb): this had been when Paton ran away. After Bartlett graduated, he asked me out to see a movie. Then he told me about Paton telling Fetter Senior he was gay, which was quite a blow only a year after Mother Fetter ran off with a wholesaler of industrial grade lubricants. Paton was the one who informed Fetter Senior about The Rock being gay, which everyone but Fetter Senior already knew, and then Fetter Senior disposed of the picture. Or maybe he hid it away somewhere, a painful treasure.

I wonder what Bartlett could be thinking now: maybe that he's only twenty years old and this is a lot to drop on a fellow, especially from the first woman he ever slept with, the first woman he ever called Girlfriend, ever heard say, "I love you." And I do love him, even though he is just a boy in a six-foot-four skeleton and size thirteen beat up boat shoes. Even though I can see he's terrified. Maybe because of that.

"There's nothing you have to do," I tell him, touching his wrists, the bones as delicate as a baby's head.

"Mara, how long have you known?"

"A month or so," I tell him. He glances toward the ceiling, calculating in his head, as if adding the cost of an all-day rental plus extra floats. And then I realize he's trying to figure out if there would still be time to open the Yellow Pages to the A's, make an appointment. So I tell him the detail that convinced me, the way water convinces the lungs not to draw air. "It was the morning of the picnic, when we went to get charcoal," I say, and Bartlett lowers his head to my open hands, and I watch his shoulder blades rise and fall as he breathes. The waitress sees us like this; she stops short, and on her tray Bartlett's beer sloshes over the rim of the plastic cup, sprinkling the basket of hushpuppies next to it. I motion for her to come over with a tick of my head. "Bartlett," I say, and he lifts his square, sad chin to look at me. I can tell he expects me to say something to comfort him, because right now he has no comfort for me; he can't even hide it. "I'm planning on Percival, boy or girl." He stares at his beer when the waitress lands it on the table. "Go ahead and bring him another one," I tell her.

MY GRANDMOTHER LOUISE came across *Mars and the Abode of Life* freshly printed from The Macmillan Company when she was sixteen and dusting shelves in a library. Then she found the earlier book, *Mars and its Canals,* and read it, too. Later, she married a man who was interested only in the price of lumber (called books a waste of pulp), and he didn't even notice eight years later when Louise began to recreate Percival Lowell's name—in reverse order since Aunt Lowell was born first in 1916, the year of her namesake's death, and then my father Percival, born in 1920, ten years before Lowell's theories of a Planet X beyond Jupiter were confirmed and my grandfather's business sank in the Depression. Contrary to my grandfather's predictions, my father didn't suffer from being named Percival; the nickname Pull came from what he'd called himself as a child. He was forty when I was born. He could judge a land's grade without instruments. He had a secret: you pretended you were looking at water and noted where and how the land varied from that flatness. My mother said this only proved he'd rather be looking at water than anything else. My father didn't dispute this. He didn't pretend to be a normal man. I remember kneeling on his lap, playing with the mechanical pencil tucked into the pocket of his short-sleeved shirt and looking into his gray-green eyes (which did appear to reflect water even as they looked at me), his eyebrows salt-and-pepper even then, his voice filling my head, reminding me, "Call me Pull, honey, like they all do."

The dream I had the night before he died went like this: I'm in front of the cottage he'd just bought, where my parents planned to retire, and he's standing at the water's edge, his back to me. He begins wading in, stepping slowly as if in a processional, the calm surface wrinkling around him. At first I think he's just walking in a little ways to fish, but he keeps going until he's in up to his neck. He begins his signature back stroke—instead of his arms pin wheeling they just flap under water like flippers, his legs slowly scissoring, the water up to his chin, his head the only thing I can see above the surface. A small wake collars his neck. I follow him in because I can't figure out why he's swimming with his clothes on; I'm worried. Then I'm no longer in the water, I am suspended above it, looking down, and I see a huge snake under the surface. "Pull!" I scream—both his name and a plea—but he just keeps paddling along. I look at the snake again and realize it's dead. I see it turning slowly as it falls toward the silty bottom. I try to tell my father all is fine again, but then he's gone, too, and there is nothing but morning-smooth water, gray as a veil.

When my father died that day, my mother refused sedatives and company. She put the cottage up for sale that very week; she sold or gave away everything we would no longer be able to use without him. This included not only his clothes, his surveying equipment, his Stan Getz albums, and his bass boat and tackle, but also her hot roller set and the dresses she wore when they went to Cotillion Cub dances. She gave me her lipsticks, frosted eyeshadow and White Shoulders perfume. She enrolled in classes a few days after the funeral.

While my mother let go of what she could no longer have, I saved what I could—a few mechanical pencils, a stray lure, and the anchor and rope that had tangled his ankles. After the ambulance left, I carried it, still wet, into the house and put it under my bed before driving my mother to the funeral home. And that was where I refused my first glass of water.

But my war with water was not realistic, I knew even then. My name means "sea," my sign is Pisces, and my element is water. Any water would do: the YWCA pool, a week at the beach, the lake where Bartlett and Paton stood eye-to-eye with The Rock and where my parents later bought a cottage—anyplace was fine. In summer my mother rubbed zinc cream into my skin because I burned like my father; it was as if we needed the shadow of water. She didn't try to get my father to wear it; he'd burned so many summers by then his freckles had simply connected. The zinc turned me even whiter; I opened my eyes in green lake water to watch my hands pulling the strokes my father showed me—breast, freestyle, side— my pale green fingers flickering like fish. And now, I am a salty ocean, home to child who knows nothing else.

BARTLETT RECOVERS. Halfway through that first beer, even. "We'll get married," he says, chomping into a hushpuppy. He grins, chewing, nodding to convince himself.

"We don't have to rush," I tell him. My father liked to say, "If it's a good idea today, won't it still be a good idea tomorrow?" He was a fan of taking one's time. He was a slow driver, always with the windows at least cracked even if it was raining, his elbow propped on the door. When I was a kid, riding with him in the front seat of the green station wagon we had then, we sang a favorite James Taylor song, "Sunny Skies." It's a catchy tune, but the words didn't make much sense to me then. *Sunny skies sleeps in the morning/ He doesn't know when to rise...Still he knows how to ease down slowly/ Everything is fine in the end/And you will be pleased to know/That sunny skies hasn't a friend.*

I loved that song. Later my mother told me it was about heroin addiction. You can love something and not understand it completely, like Fetter Senior's autographed headshot of The Rock, or Lowell's carefully recorded canals. I hold Bartlett's hand and wonder how my mother and especially Aunt Lowell will react when I tell them. The universe is expanding, I'll explain. There's room for this baby, this new family.

AFTER LUNCH DURING THE WEEK, my mother works in the community college information office, directing calls. Aunt Lowell takes a nap in the afternoons. I walk to work at the Suds & Duds and stay until nine. But today is Sunday, and we're all here.

My mother has a big algebra test tomorrow, which she plans to study for at the library once it opens at one. Aunt Lowell wants me to take her to the grocery, but it doesn't open until noon. She says she likes me to drive and needs my help loading the groceries. But it's also because of the way we've agreed to handle finances. Mom pays the utilities and part of the rent, and I pay for the groceries. The idea is to make sure Aunt Lowell spends less while we're living with her. Aunt Lowell has no problem handing the electric, gas, and phone bill over to my mother; I often find them fanned artfully on the bed if I get home from work before my mother returns from studying. But she doesn't seem to want to ask me for money, even though I know it would be a burden to feed three when her pension barely covers one. So if I go with her, I can simply offer to pay, and it's a nicety we have—my offer, her surprised acceptance at the register, every week.

Aunt Lowell and I are making a list and my mother is trying to solve word problems. "How am I supposed to care about this?" she says. "Two idiots driving separately to a park twelve kilometers away? Who thinks in kilometers? And why wouldn't they ride together?" My mother looks at me and Aunt Lowell across the round kitchen table.

Aunt Lowell blinks once. "You're not supposed to try to understand the problem, you're just supposed to use the information to structure the equation."

My mother consults her textbook as if to find something with which to contradict Aunt Lowell. Aunt Lowell catches my eye and winks. I know she'd love to tell my mother who thinks in kilometers. Once she took me with her to a teacher's convention in Washington, DC. She'd won an award for her teaching. We rode the Southern Crescent and slept in bunks barely as wide as my nine-year-old shoulders. We went to the top of the Washington Monument and she told me to look toward the other end of the

Mall. "If the sun was the Capital," she'd said, "Lowell's Pluto would be about here, with us, and the Earth would be at that carousel, probably," she said, pointing to the spinning red top, toy-sized bright horses flashing beneath the cherry-blossomed trees. "Imagine how far he had to look. Five-point-nine billion kilometers." She didn't translate the number into miles. She'd expected me to know.

"Are you putting some wine on the list this time?" my mother asks.

"Why don't you get what you like?" Aunt Lowell says. "I wouldn't know."

My mother eyes me. This is an ongoing tension, the grocery list. I'm not much of a drinker myself, and of course right now I'm not drinking at all. I know she likes Chardonnay, and in truth she almost never drinks more than a glass a night. But my grandfather had eased his business woes with whiskey, erasing the family's savings in a few short years. This is why Aunt Lowell went to the teacher's college on scholarship and then straight to work. I've never seen her take even a sip of alcohol. I tip my head just slightly to tell my mother yes, I'll get the wine.

But my mother isn't ready to let it drop. "I'm sure you haven't noticed, with your busy schedule, that I don't have a lot of time to shop," she says to Aunt Lowell, in a dig at her retirement.

Aunt Lowell sits up straighter in her chair. "It doesn't surprise me that your course load requires a lot of study time on your part, Doris. The question I have is whether you're doing it for the right reasons."

Now my mother is straightening up in her chair, too, shoulders squared. I've never been clear on why they don't get along. Sometimes I think Aunt Lowell believes my mother wasn't good enough for my father because she didn't go to college and didn't like to read. To give them both credit, neither has spoken badly of the other to me. I'll admit I've hoped lately that they would become friends through our shared loss, a small good from the worst thing that could have happened to any of us.

My mother snaps closed her textbook and stands up. Its title is *Modern Algebra*, as if there's an ancient one covered in another course. "My husband is dead and I have to think about my reasons?"

Here, I'm thinking this might be a good time to give them my news. I've of course worried—expected—that they'd be unhappy about it. But I can't gather my thoughts fast enough to steer Aunt Lowell away from what I know she's going to say as soon as my mother mentions my father.

"You seem to be over your husband, Doris, if your study habits are any indication," Aunt Lowell says.

They stare at each other for a moment, eyes narrowed. My mother picks up her book, and as she turns to pound out of the room, she looks at me for only a moment. But it's long enough. I've betrayed her, and she knows it. The apartment rattles with her footfalls. I look at Aunt Lowell, waiting for her to return my gaze. But she doesn't. She pretends to review her list until my mother slams the apartment door behind her and we hear her footsteps echoing, then fading, in the hall.

"You didn't have to say anything about that," I tell her.

"I know," she says. She rests her elbows on the table and props her forehead on her cupped palms. "I miss him," she says, and her shoulders tremble, and she is crying, fat tear drops on our grocery list. I want to feel bad for her, but I don't. The worst betrayal is that you have to go on when you lose someone; this is what I've come to realize. Nothing is preserved. You have to pay the bills and make grocery lists; you have to let other people love you in place of the one who's gone.

What happened was I got sent home early from the Suds & Duds because there wasn't any more folding work, and it only takes one person to monitor the machines and give change. It was late afternoon a few weeks ago in early July, right before I figured out I was pregnant. My mother had just started school and already she was staying in the library until dinnertime nearly every day, preparing for the next day's classes. She'd told me she liked to study on the third floor, where it was quiet, and that was where I could always find her if she wasn't in class or at the switchboard. So I took the stairs and skirted the stacks. I saw her first, her back to me, head bent in concentration, it seemed, over a book. But as I got to the end of the stacks, I saw a boy about my age sitting across the table from her, his fingers resting on the back of her hand. I had time to notice that the half-moons of his nails were black with grease, and a pack of cigarettes was tucked in his T-shirt pocket. His brown hair looked as if it had been cut with broken scissors, ragged over the ears and the back of his skinny neck. Then he looked up at me, and that made my mother turn, and when she saw me she did not seem embarrassed that I'd seen her with this boy's hand resting on hers. She stood up and then he stood and smiled I could see his teeth were already turning yellow from the cigarettes, and the shine on his forehead made me want to wash his face. He told me he worked in his father's body shop, banging out accidents from bumpers and doors, and that he was studying to be an engineer. If he said his name, I immediately forgot it. Through all this, my mother seemed calm, even cheerful, but when he said the part about being an engineer I looked at her, and she looked at her hands, as if wondering how the boy's fingertips had come to rest there, as if surprised by the glint of her gold wedding band in the light of a humid afternoon.

But what had I seen? A moment of comfort—maybe after she'd told the boy about her husband? I remembered their heads bent together right before the boy looked up, questioning. He looked younger than Bartlett though he'd said he was twenty-four. I didn't believe anything was going on—if I'd wanted to wash the boy's face, she must've thought the same thing, having actually washed a child's face thousands of times.

It was her lack of discomfort at seeing me that had led me to mention it to Aunt Lowell. Or maybe it was a desire to make the best of what I had seen, whatever it was, to confer innocence by acting as if it were casual enough to mention to anyone. That same afternoon, when I got home from seeing my mother and the boy in the library, Aunt Lowell had just gotten up from her nap; she was sitting at the kitchen table, sipping her red iced tea and gazing out the window. I told her about getting off work early and stopping by to find my mother in the library.

"What does she do up there all by herself?" Aunt Lowell asked, an odd question, I thought, from a teacher who'd expected a lot of study hours from her students.

"She's studying with someone from her class," I said.

"Someone?" Aunt Lowell said, interest lighting her pale blue eyes.

I wouldn't have said anything if Aunt Lowell hadn't asked about my mother being by herself. "He's going to be an engineer, so I guess he's a good algebra partner."

Aunt Lowell turned back to the window. I wanted to clarify, but I felt anything I said would convince her further that something significant hadn't been said. Aunt Lowell respected a woman's independence—hers granted by no choice of her own, working to support herself—but she also thought a respectable woman had no need to sit in libraries alone in the evening when she had a home to come to. Maybe she was thinking of her own mother, giving up the dusty, breathing library shelves, which housed her dreams of starlit Martian canals, for a marriage as airless as space.

"WE'LL MOVE OUT," my mother tells me at breakfast the next morning while Aunt Lowell is in the shower. The plumbing croons like a lonely bird. She looks tired, her dark eyes shadowed, squinting. I didn't even hear her come in the night before; she stayed away for the rest of the afternoon and evening, and I fell asleep right after dinner because these days sleep unrolls itself on me like a heavy blanket.

I swallow my mouthful of cereal, look at my bowl. "I'm sorry," I say. "I only mentioned I'd seen you, and she took it wrong."

My mother waves my words away. "We can make it," she says. "Easily. I'll just take fewer classes in the fall and work more. Or I'll just work full time and you can take classes. The students are coming back so we need to look for a place now."

"Mom, she misunderstood, that's all."

My mother looks at me. She rests her hand on mine the same way that boy did with her. "His name is Walter Lambertson," she said.

"I never thought—" I start, but she keeps going.

"He's smaller than Pull. But his voice is similar, and the way he picks up a pen. You know what I'm talking about, don't you? How gentle he was with everything?"

My mother is crying now, her lips pressed into a grim line. "I thought the best thing was to cut away everything I could, and let it heal over. But I heard that boy talking in class and now he's my study partner. I don't care what this means to anyone. I married your father when I was twenty-three and now I'm forty-five and I have to tell you something, Mara. The world has split open for me. I will not apologize for anything I want to do. I'm moving out as soon as I can find a place, with or without you."

This proclamation has calmed her; she wipes her eyes with her knuckles and sips her orange juice. We always add an extra can of water to the frozen concentrate to make it last longer. Maybe we thought these careful measures would protect us from harm or loss, or at least I did. I didn't think much would be asked of me, living in that cottage with my parents on a small brown lake, watching Puddle's Paddle Boats passing slowly and my father casting off the dock. I'd finished high school and I was working in a Laundromat and I was in love with a boy. I smelled of steam and detergent and sex, and I was in no hurry to move out. Pull wasn't worried about it. Maybe he wanted me to stay because he was afraid I would settle for Bartlett, renting paddle boats with his loud father. "I waited late to do my best work, too," he'd say, kissing me on top of my head as he cleared dishes after dinner. My mother would shake her head, but smile, and I sat with her as she finished her wine at the table. We were living in my father's dream, a house on the water. I believed there was enough room in it for all of us, indefinitely.

Behind me, Aunt Lowell strides into the kitchen with her businesslike heel-toe. She's wearing a red pantsuit, her strawberry blonde hair slicked back, some curls already escaping. It will dry into a fine cloud at her crown. I turn to her and she smiles at me before busying herself with filling the kettle for her tea. She pretends not to see my mother. In return, my mother manages to project a complete unawareness of Aunt Lowell's presence as well. I wait until the kettle is full before I speak.

"I'm pregnant."

I can hear Aunt Lowell taking in a breath. My mother catches my eye first, her own eyes widening as the meaning of the words take hold for her. "Have you been to a doctor?" she asks.

"I had a test at Planned Parenthood," I say.

"Have you—?" she begins, but then she stops herself, pushes to her feet, palms flat on the table, and comes around to hug my head to her chest the way she used to do when I'd scraped my knee.

Then I can hear Aunt Lowell behind me, and my mother reluctantly steps back, allowing Aunt Lowell to envelop me in her own damp, talcum-scented hug. I'm surprised—I didn't know how she'd react, given her life as a career woman and her disdain for Bartlett. I'd wondered if the title of intelligence she'd conferred on me would suddenly be withdrawn. She asks the due date, and I tell her, and all seems to be going well—Aunt Lowell and my mother even smile at each other from the opposite shores of the table, but then my mother shoots down Aunt Lowell's suggestion of a celebratory lunch today at the cafeteria. "Don't you think this is worth a dinner out, maybe, someplace nice?" my mother says, an accusing lilt in her tone.

Both of them look at me, certain I will choose their side. I wish there was some way to make them both happy, given the fact that happiness has been in short supply for all of us lately. But like my mother, I will no longer apologize for what I want. I tell them, "I want to get ice cream at the lake and ride the paddleboats this weekend." I take one of each of their hands. "I want you to meet Fetter Senior," I say to Aunt Lowell, and I look back at my mother before Aunt Lowell's shoulders wilt further in disappointment. My mother has already turned her eyes to the floor. Neither she nor Aunt Lowell, who never shared Pull's love for water, have been to the lake since the cottage was sold. "Don't you think it's time?" I ask, but I'm not surprised when neither of them responds. I squeeze their hands and let go.

In the bathroom, I undress and step into the shower. I watch the warm water roll down my belly. I feel it then: a wave of movement, maybe only a ripple, like a question.

"We're going to be fine," I say, and for now I have no choice but to believe it.

WOULD IT HAVE BEEN BETTER had I been there, like my mother, looking up from the kitchen window to see only the boat in the water, drifting? Then running out to the dock to see how the anchor line dragged the boat down on one side, then screaming for him when it became clear there was only one place he could be?

Is it better to be the discoverer, like Lowell, or the one who has to live with what's known?

I'd gone with Bartlett to buy charcoal. It was May, but the spring had been rainy and cool, the lake still holding winter. Pull figured at least some of the fish had burrowed out of the silk mud of the banks, sensing the coming warmth even from that soft lake floor. He was planning to grill that afternoon.

Bartlett drove. He knows the tree-fringed shore better than even my father, simply because he'd grown up on this water, watching other people conquer it in Easter-egg-colored boats. He knows where the unmapped gravel roads dwindle to small clearings where fires are built, the catch eaten a few feet from shore. On the way back from the grocery, we stopped at one of those piney coves, and

I slipped my underwear off under my skirt and slid across the front seat and straddled him. There was the smell of lake in his hair as always, and I could also smell a trace of gear lubricant on his hands when he lifted my hair off my neck—this was before I cut it—along with the bitter smell of the charcoal from the back seat. I rode Bartlett, who always keeps his eyes open until he comes, and then he looks prayerful. As he tipped his head back and tensed, eyes closed now, gratefully, I realized I hadn't even paid attention to my own body. I had been thinking, oddly, of effortlessness, in letting things present themselves, in taking one's time. I was not thinking I'd get pregnant so soon after my period.

Pull was dying right then. My mother might have been screaming for him even as Bartlett and I rested in the car, though I like to think I might have heard her voice, thin, over the water. Later, it could not be absolutely determined if the heart attack started first, causing him to lose his balance, his foot tangling in the anchor line as he fell, or whether he'd simply tripped, got tangled up somehow, and the cold water triggered the heart attack, not enough to kill him on land, but enough so that he could not swim.

I would not go inside the house, as the EMTs requested, before they lifted him from the water. I stood with my mother on the dock, and I saw his face, white as bone, and his arm flung out to one side, and the anchor hanging from his ankle. Bartlett stood on the shore, Fetter Senior pacing and muttering behind him, not far from the ambulance, as if this had been a mistake someone should have been held accountable for. In the yelling and confusion, I felt my mother's body tightening like a coiled snake. We had seen the end of the world.

THE NIGHT BEFORE MY FIRST appointment with Dr. Finch, who delivered me, I dream of my father again. But in this dream, he's a little boy of about three or four, and I'm supposed to watch him. We're on a beach. Behind us is a four-room house on stilts behind the dunes and a power line stitching the sky. This is where in waking life my family used to vacation in the summer. There's no one else around.

I walk with my boy-father to the ocean, and he plays in the water. The waves are very strong, so I watch him closely. Then I notice he's growing younger and smaller, to the point where he can't even stand up anymore, can't run from the waves crashing over him. I pick him up and carry him back to the house and hold him in the dark bedroom. By now he is an infant, lying very still in my arms. I look down at him. I realize he has gone so far back in time that his soul is leaving him.

When I wake up, I'm sweating and my belly is tight—not a cramp but a balling, like a closing fist. I'm in the guest bedroom; my mother had insisted I take the bed. I have to look around the room for several seconds to place myself—the dark wood ceiling fan with the frosted glass tulip-shaped light fixture, the dresser with the silver-framed oval mirror hung above it, the three lace doilies on top of the hope chest my grandmother had made for Aunt Lowell's trousseau, which never graced a marriage bed. "Help me," I whisper, because in that moment I'm still not completely sure where I am. The balling tightens again and then I yell it.

The three of us shuffle down the steps in a gasping clump. My mother drives Aunt Lowell's car. She's supposed to have a test this morning, but she says only some schedules are worth keeping, and I think of Wally Lambertson waiting for her, his pencil cradled thoughtfully over a page. She makes me lie down in the back seat, and because I'm still sweating, my hair sticking to my face from sleep, she rolls the windows down, and I feel I'm in the green station wagon again, sailing. From this point of view, all I can see are tree tops, power lines, the points of only the tallest roofs, and a band of blue sky. Aunt Lowell is turned halfway around in the passenger seat, holding my hand and patting it. I curl on my side, thighs squeezed together. I palm the small mound of my belly like a host with her hand on the door frame, not wanting the guest to leave.

Dr. Finch told my mother he'd meet us at the hospital. When we get to the emergency entrance, Aunt Lowell runs inside, and my mother opens the back car door and helps me sit up. Mostly I am dizzy from riding lying down, but the balling in my belly is even stronger. I grip the edge of the seat cushion. "I remember," I breathe, trying to concentrate and distract us both at the same time. She is bent toward me, holding the car door open with her hip, reaching for me. "Pull and I used to sing that James Taylor song." I can't remember the title or any of the words right then, so I try to hum it.

My mother squats in front of me, cups my sweaty cheeks, her thumbs running under my eyes. "Honey, that was our song," she said. "I sang that to you all the time." She stands and bends again, this time to slide her arms under mine and lift me to my feet. I am crying without effort; the tears spill from my eyes and roll down my nose as I lean against her, head propped on her shoulder, and we are met by a nurse and a wheelchair and Aunt Lowell and the breeze of air conditioning, and I let them wheel me inside.

In the pale green hospital room, Dr. Finch gives me a painkiller and hooks me to a drip to slow the contractions. My eyes half-closed, gummy, I listen to him tell me and my mother and Aunt Lowell that there is life in there yet. "We've had a scare," he says. "We'll have to watch carefully."

Then he is gone, and my mother and aunt crouch on either side my bed at my hips. Their faces hover on the edge of my focus—Aunt Lowell a pink cloud, my mother a dark moon. I get the feeling that they want me to tell them what to do, but the drugs garble my words. "How about Bartlett," I say, meaning, "Would you call Bartlett, please?" and then, "Find the beauty in us," and I'm not sure what I meant by that at all, but it seems to send them into a careful orbit, rising from the bed together, drifting to the door and beyond the range of my darkening vision.

IN AUNT LOWELL'S LIVING ROOM hangs a small framed print of Percival Lowell peering into the telescope he built at the observatory on

Mars Hill. He sits in the observer's chair—a small kitchen chair, really, from the looks of it, on a square platform attached to a ladder-like lift on wheels. Behind him, the circular room is finished in narrow horizontal paneling. He wears a dark three-piece suit, white cuff-linked shirt, and beret. Because the telescope's mount isn't shown, it looks as if the entire instrument rests on Lowell's eye at its tiniest point.

When I come to, this print is propped at my bedside, the first thing I see, and once again I can't remember where I am. Then I hear someone draw in a breath, and I can tell even before I turn my head that it's Bartlett from the patient way he coaxes air into his lungs. We look at each other in the green, filmy light. I can almost feel the cool sting of lake water against my eyeballs.

"I'm supposed to work tonight," I say, trying to sit up.

"It's tomorrow, and you're supposed to go home," Bartlett says.

It takes a moment for this to sink in. "I was going to go to the lake today, then."

Bartlett takes my hand. His long face is serious. "Maybe tomorrow."

I place my other hand on my belly. "Do I still have it?"

Bartlett leans to kiss my knuckles. "Yes," he says. "We do."

THAT WEEKEND, in the early evening after dinner, my mother drives again, this time to the lake, Aunt Lowell in the passenger seat and me in the back. I am wearing blue terry cloth shorts and a bell-shaped peach cotton maternity shirt that my mother dug out of the bottom of a box, one of the few things that survived our former lives. In my canvas tote, in a plastic bag, is the anchor, which I'd stored in the brick garage at Aunt Lowell's place, finding its dull gleam under the dirt-smeared garage windows.

Fetter Senior slaps the counter when I walk in to Puddle's Paddle Boat Rentals. Aunt Lowell and my mother follow. "There's my future daughter-in-law," he bellows, working his way around the register to hug me. He pats me hard between the shoulders and my forehead bumps against a sweaty drape of neck stubble. I don't even look back at Aunt Lowell or my mother; I can feel their disdain tingling on my scalp. "Hey!" he yells through the square, screenless window to Bartlett, "Get in here!"

Though he offers no reason, Bartlett complies, walking swiftly down the dock and out of view for a moment, shoulders curled inward as I'd seen him do for years, before we knew each other. Fetter Senior turns to Aunt Lowell and my mother. "Doris," Fetter Senior says, as gently as he's able, though if you had only his tone of voice to go on and not his quickly lowered eyes, thick hands clasped over his belly, you wouldn't realize he's trying to sound comforting. My mother looks away. He turns then to Aunt Lowell, whom he met at the funeral, but it's clear he doesn't remember her.

"How do you do," she says, her gaze straying to Fetter Senior's collection of celebrity photos on the back wall, all those black-framed, smiling faces—Ava Gardner, Bob Hope, Johnny Carson.

He bustles back behind the counter. "Just got a new one," he says, as Bartlett appears in the doorway. "Hi everyone," Bartlett says to us, nearly bowing to my mother and Aunt Lowell. They regard him with similar expressions, somewhere between irritation and disappointment. On this, at least, they can agree. When they left Bartlett and me alone in the hospital room two days earlier, it was not just to give us privacy, I'm certain, but because they haven't quite reconciled themselves to the fact that this lanky, long-chinned boy-man is the father of our next generation.

"Burt Reynolds," Fetter Senior nearly shouts, thrusting the framed and signed headshot to me first for inspection. Burt Reynolds has sideburns and glossy black hair and a dark-eyed gaze. He smiles at you as if he already knows some bad guy is going to try to kick his ass, like in *Smokey and the Bandit*, but you'll be the one to save him. "Now there's a real man," Fetter Senior says, pointing. "He is what he is. No playing pansy."

Bartlett's biting his lip. This is what he does when he wants to say something but decides not to. He bites his lip a lot around Fetter Senior. I do it, too, in sympathy, staring at Burt's dark eyes, and right then it occurs to me Paton looked a lot like him. A ninety-five-pound version, true, but with the same thick eyebrows that curve up at the bridge of his nose, so it looks like he's laughing at a joke he knows better than to share. I also realize that Fetter Senior, minus a few dozen pounds, wouldn't look all that different than Burt, and that Paton took after him, and perhaps that is why his son had to disappear.

I hand Burt back over. "Did you see him in *Deliverance?*" I ask. "Great movie." I say it for Paton, and for Bartlett, but when I see Fetter Senior's pained pinch of a frown, I'm sorry for it. *Your son isn't dead*, I want to say to him. The difference is important: disappointment or loss. A breeze drifts through the unscreened window and I can smell the lake—suspended silt and fish and sweet rot—just like always.

Fetter Senior recovers quickly. "Let's get you a boat," he says.

Aunt Lowell shakes her head. "I'll wait at the picnic tables," she says. But Fetter Senior will have none of it. He claps an arm around her shoulders and herds her to the door. Aunt Lowell presses against his arm in protest, but from the back it appears she is swooning in his embrace. I look at my mother and catch her quick smile. She may not want to be here, but she enjoys Aunt Lowell's not wanting to be here even more.

Bartlett squires us into a sun-faded red paddleboat one by one. Aunt Lowell sits with him in front; my mother and I ride in back. I place my tote between my mother's and my feet. Bartlett's skin glows, sunburned, in the soft evening light. He clears his throat, paddling along as he turns to Aunt Lowell. "I've set up the telescope," he says to her. "Should be perfect viewing in a little while, before the moonrise."

Good for you, I think to Bartlett.

Aunt Lowell watches the barely threaded wake in the water. "I don't know how long we'll stay." But her wistful tone tells me the lake calm is already soothing her.

Beside me, my mother appears not to have heard. She is gazing at our cottage, which looks so much smaller to me across the water than it felt on the inside, the huge picture window only a glint from this distance.

I wait until we're even with the dock and the boathouse where my father stood for hours in the evening, the water whispering to him. I open my tote and slide the anchor from the plastic bag, rest its cool weight in my lap. The crinkling plastic gets my mother's attention. "What's that?" she says.

I wait to give her time to see for herself. She looks up at me, recognizing it.

Aunt Lowell turns, alerted by the edge in my mother's voice. She follows her stare, but I can tell she's confused by the curved piece of metal, not being the water person Pull was.

I say to them, "I thought we could put it back."

My mother falls back against the plastic seat, eyes closed, arms crossed.

I say, "I've blamed everything I can think of—water, charcoal, dreams, myself for not being there."

She turns her head back and forth slowly. "We've all done that."

I know I could say the name of the boy from the library to her and she'd understand: none of us have let go. I wait for her to say something else, to look at me. We are all silent, floating under the darkening sky. After a while, my mother reaches for the horseshoe curve of lead, slowly, as if moving through water. She cups it gently as a child's cheek. Then she takes her hand away and folds her fingers together in her lap.

I cradle the anchor over the skin of the water. Aunt Lowell reaches for my mother's shoulder, pats her. I see Bartlett from the corner of my eye, feel the paddleboat dip as he turns toward me, as he watches me bend with the weight of our past life. The lake takes the anchor with a gulp—water folding over itself and then smoothing.

After a moment, Bartlett says, "That's it." But he's not looking at the water anymore. His face tilts skyward, the first starlight white on the ridge of his forehead. He points to a steady red point of light just above the dark tree line.

We all look. My mother sits up, wiping her cheeks with the back of her hand. Aunt Lowell sighs. I remember the triumph in her voice that day we stood high above the Mall, telling me the distance of her namesake's imagination.

"It's getting closer, you know, in its orbit," Bartlett says.

"People will go there," Aunt Lowell says. "They'll find water, just like Lowell predicted." Her pale round face gazes upward.

"He never wanted to be without it," my mother says. But of course she's talking about my father, measuring with his steady, gray-green eyes the earth against the flatness of water. I think he could've helped Lowell on a clear night like this. He might have told him those hoped-for canals were just a reflection of all we'd ever wanted and lost.

Bartlett begins to turn us back toward home. The paddles churn and thump, and I see the last glow of evening on the water, and imagine us in a ship, sailing over our anchor as it comes to rest on the silty earth. Across the lake, in front of the yellow boathouse lights, I see Fetter Senior standing on the dock, a backlit shadow, waiting for us to return safely to land.

Small

Roy's not. But the word's out on his box, and now they call him *li'l bit* at school. He thought he could deal, but then Hector—*his friend*—called it a doll house, and Roy blanked after *take it back*, and now Hector's got a cracked rib and a busted ear drum, and after that it doesn't matter that last summer Roy carried Hector's little brother up eight flights of steps to their mama when he cut his cheek open trying to clear a fire hydrant on his bike. Or that Hector and Roy go way back, staying in the same four-room cribs, just on different floors, the projects like fat square monsters up on the hill, gonna crush them.

Hector's mama called Roy a menace. Now Roy's mama got to get to the school after her nightwatch job and ask the principal can Roy come back. *Send me begging*, his mama say. *You want that?* She's down there now, and Roy's waiting.

Roy's bother Damen says motherfucker had it coming. Roy's sister Tamika says he better watch his crazy self if he wants to get anywhere in this life. She brought him the notebook, helped him make his house pictures look real. Perspective. Means things up close are large and things far away are small. And everything comes to a point. She wrote it in his notebook, and he copied it until it seemed like something he could say.

Wood crate came from a Dumpster. Roy sprayed it red, painted windows too with Wite-Out he stole from Ms. Fulson's desk. Inside, matchbox beds in all four bedrooms with dishrag bedspreads, everybody gets one. Pictures on the cardboard walls cut from magazines. One of Tamika's glitter earrings for a hanging lamp. Big-screen TV (old eye shadow box from his mama) in the living room.

Roy's looking, planning for what to add next, when his mama come in crying. Says he got to go to special ed. *For motional problems.*

Motional? Roy's got no problem with motion. He raises his arms straight out. He's flying over the house in a plane. He's seeing everybody in there now, happy. Everything small because it's so far away.

Trigger Finger

THIRTEEN AND PREGNANT. Fact of it is, she's a wild child. I'd guess she's five months gone, but a little looks like a lot on her stick frame. There she is, not ten feet away from me, lying on the concrete stoop in this July heat on her side, looking asleep but her eyes are open. Not a word when I say hello. She's wearing white shorts and a red halter top. Her belly's a huge peach poking over her waistband. There's a plate with some bread crusts sitting a few inches in front of her face, like someone thought to feed her like a dog. Her head rests on the crook of one of her bony arms. A fat black fly lands on a crust. She doesn't shoo it, but it takes off anyway in a dizzy circle and lands on her hip. It's still there when I go back inside from smoking my cigarette.

There's four of them living up in that little apartment—the girl, her brother, her mother, and her mother's boyfriend, though he's only there sometimes, so maybe he doesn't count. At first, I wondered where they all slept—did one of the kids get the couch? But lately it seems to me they never sleep. Screaming and crying at all hours, doors slamming, things flung against walls. The whole damn building shaking. I never knew white people could be so loud.

Like tonight. Or this morning, call it. I wake up at three-thirty to a cat meowing, more like howling, just outside my window. I figure it to be one of those strays living in the woods behind my apartment, and I pull my robe over my nightgown and come down the hall to the linen closet, where I also keep my broom and mop.

I get the broom and round the corner to the living room, planning to go out the front door and come around the side of the house to knock the thing off my window. That window is painted shut, so there's no other way to do it. Going out at this hour of the night, combined with having to confront some animal, when I'm not an animal person, makes my skin tingle all over.

But when I get to the living room, the sound shifts, and I realize it wasn't coming through my window but the wall between my apartment and the neighbors. At first, because I'm still half-asleep, I think one of the cats must've somehow gotten in between the walls, like squirrels can do. They're skinny enough. But when it wails again, I know it's not any cat at all, but the girl. It's got to be her. I step closer, between my TV and armchair, to listen. I hear a thump low on the wall, and I realize she's leaning against it, maybe sitting on the floor. I touch my hand to the wall when she cries again, a low moan, and I wonder if she's gone into labor. That'd be the best thing for her, ask me; her hips don't seem wide enough to pass a newborn's head. When her moan starts again, I tap the wall, just three times, right where I think her head might be. The sound stops. I don't hear anything for a minute. Then a rustle as she moves away.

I sit there listening, but I can't figure what I'd do if I heard anything more. If I call the cops, they'll know it was me. The apartment on the other side of them is empty. I'm too awake to get back in bed, so I turn on the TV with the sound low. *Crazy*, I think. It could've been the mother crying. But the whine was too high, like a child. Any woman who's had her own baby would know that sound.

It's almost dawn by the time I fall asleep on the couch, and then I only get an hour or two. By the time Louis pulls around back in his Jeep Cherokee, I've had a shower, coffee and a couple aspirin, but my head aches almost as bad as when I still drank.

"Whyn't you call me?" he says, which is what he always says when I complain. He has to duck his head to step through the door. He's near a foot taller than me. I've always liked big men; and he's that: arms as thick as my thighs, a huge chest and a heavy jaw. White people's scared to death of him. You'd think he could have some fun with that, but it's brought him trouble. So he moves cheerful as you please through a store or a parking lot, especially at night. He nods at everyone he sees. He doesn't wear no trashy gangster clothes. He knows I'm not the only woman in town with a gun. He knows all it'd take is some white woman thinking he aims to rape her and his black ass could be blown away.

I've been raped. I know what to be scared of. For me it was four white guys jumping me when I got off from a waitress job, sixteen years old. They broke a bottle and shoved it up in me and left me to bleed to death. But I didn't.

I take a look through the front window to see if Miss Pregnant is holding court on the stoop again. No one there. "You want to get in the middle of other people's problems?"

"I'd set 'em straight."

He's shutting the door behind him and locking it, they way I like it, chain and all. I look up at him, ready to say he must be crazy; if they's that bad to each other, what's he think they'll do to him? But when he turns around, he's smiling, and he opens his arms and I step into them, and he smells like soap and cologne, and I think, like I almost always do at least once every time I'm with him, that all the things that have happened in my life, even some of the worst, have led me to him. He is my reward on earth.

Louis wants me to go with him to see how some carpet samples look in his house. He bought it after a wall fell on him at a construction site and broke his back. He got a lawyer on contingency, and the lawyer figured out someone hadn't bolted the wall right, which was against code. He paid off his mother's house, too, and still had some to put in the bank. He's doing all right. Now he only limps when he's tired.

"I've been talking to Sarah about her moving out," he says once we're driving. He doesn't look at me because he knows this is a sore point. Almost as soon as he bought that house, his sister started begging to move in with her three kids. Just for a while, she told him. Here she was between jobs, all alone. Like her husband left her yesterday instead of before the first kid was even born. Like those other two kids by two different men don't say something about why she can't get a man now. And then she's all the time whining about how high the utilities are, when she doesn't even pay a dime in rent.

Meanwhile, here Louis is, living with his mama. What good is having a house if you can't even live in it? But. The only reason he came back down here at all was because he'd split from his wife. If he hadn't been working down here, that wall wouldn't have fallen on him, and maybe he wouldn't have called me. That's what I think about when I remember how the phone rang one evening and, when I answered, he said in that voice I'd never forgotten, that voice like honey pouring over wood, "What's happening, Lullaby?" No one else ever called me that. I hadn't heard from him in thirty years.

I pull myself back to the moment. "She gonna do it?"

He nods, winks at me. "What colors you like anyway?" he asks, and there can be no mistaking what all this is adding up to. I think of the twenty-odd years I've lived alone, since I came back from detox when my son was ten. I think of all the times I wondered what happened to Louis after he left. Most women would fall all over a man like him. Maybe I should count myself lucky. But I don't feel lucky yet. I feel nervous.

"You ought to get those kids out before you put down any new carpet."

Louis rolls his eyes and shakes his head. He knows where this talk can go. Part of the reason he let his sister live in his house all this time was because until just before he looked me up, he was driving up to Jersey whenever he could, even with his back on fire, trying to get back together with Karina. Maybe he hoped his broken back would make her take pity. Maybe he hoped his daughters would beg him to stay. He hoped wrong.

But from the corner of my eye, I can see him today just as he was: Tony's sweet-faced cousin who brought Cedric and me food when Tony had left us on one of his drunks. Out in that shack, in those dark woods. Sometimes he'd stay past when I put Cedric to bed. Then he might pull out some beer or some shine, and we'd drink it warm out on that rickety front porch, moonlight slipping through the seams of the roof. He never tried to touch me. But I wanted him to. The drink took me out of my body, which I guess I always wanted some kind of escape from, after what had happened to me. Louis knew, but he never said. He never said, and he never touched me, and I always thought that was why.

"That girl next door," I say when we turn down the road to his—*his sister's*—house. "She's pregnant." I wasn't sure before. But seeing her yesterday, there was no doubt. It's like her belly popped out all at once.

"That little kid?" he says, frowning as slows for the driveway. He's seen her horsing around. He called her stray cat, like those ones out back that scatter when I put out the trash, shooting like flame over the gravel.

"She was laying out on the front stoop all day. You missed it."

"Somebody ought to call Social Services," Louis says.

"Louis, that girl was sashaying up and down the street like she was selling it from Day One. It was bound to happen." I don't mean to sound harsh, but I know how the world works. If a woman—or a girl—shakes it around like she's offering, someone's bound to take her up on it. May not be fair, but it's the way things are.

But Louis is probably thinking of his daughters up there in Jersey, maybe with too much time on their hands while their momma's working. He parks and cuts the engine. "Ain't no girl that age know what she's getting herself into. The law says she was raped even if she tore off her clothes and begged for it. You know that. You should call."

I unbuckle my seatbelt slow, just to have something to do to calm myself. I don't know why this is getting to me. Maybe it's because he seems to think I believe this girl deserves what happened to her. I don't believe that anymore than I think I deserved it. Maybe it's how he said *You know that*, like since I was foolish enough to let myself get jumped, I should be an expert on these things now.

"Maybe she wants the baby," I snap as Louis gets out. He comes around to my side to help me out, because it's a long way down for me. His fingertips are warm on my wrists. "Anyway," I say, "too late to do anything about it."

Louis presses his lips together as he opens the back end of the Jeep. I feel weak somehow. Why don't I even want to make a phone call for this girl? Maybe because she's white, so in my opinion she's got a hell of a lot more going for her without doing anything. And she's so sullen-looking. Like she don't want my help or anyone's. But then I hear myself saying to Louis that I'll call. He smiles then, pulling out those carpet samples. He asks me if I can carry a couple, and I say yes. Sometimes I think that's all I can say to him: yes, yes, yes.

I follow him up the front walk, and already I'm irritated again. Plastic toys all over the place, dirt patches in the lawn. He rings the doorbell, which I think is a shame, him having to ask permission to come in his own house.

Sarah's oldest, Nico, opens up. "Uncle Louie here!" he screams over his shoulder, and then he runs off, leaving us standing there with the door open.

Louis waits for me to go in first, and then he steps inside behind me. The grimy vinyl in the foyer makes me mad, and the crooked furniture, and the dishes all over the breakfast table in the kitchen. It's not like it's my house, but maybe I'm already seeing it that way. *Watch yourself*, I think.

His sister calls out from the back. "I'm getting dressed!" Nico comes flying down the hallway again, followed by Thomas. I guess the baby must be sleeping, if that's possible with all the shrieking. The boys jump on Louis at the same time, one on each leg. He drops the carpet squares to the floor and walks around like Frankenstein, growling and reaching down to tickle them, until they fall off and roll on their backs, laughing. They're almost cute like that, but when they look at me, I narrow my eyes to make sure they keep their distance. They jump on him again.

"Go on out," he says, lurching over to the sliding glass doors that open onto the little patio in back. "Go on and I'll be out in a minute." Somehow those kids listen to him. They sure as hell don't listen to Sarah. Louis bends, reaching for one of the squares, and then straightens, pressing at the bottom of his spine with both hands.

"You shouldn't be doing that crazy stuff with those kids," I say. I reach down before he has the chance to try again and I spread each square out. They're all shades of beige, but one is grayish, one has some pink, one is more yellow, and one is a little green.

I know immediately that I like the gray one best, but I straighten up and walk back and forth looking at them, trying to act like none of them really appeal.

"Take off your shoes," he says.

"What?"

He catches me looking down the hall. "What you worried about?" He puts the toe of his left shoe up against the heel of his right and steps out of it. "You can't pick out carpet without walking on it in your bare feet." He gets his other shoe off and then sits on the end of the couch to peel off his socks.

I wonder if he's gone crazy. "I'm not taking off my panty hose, now."

"Close enough," he says. He tries out my favorite one first. I step out of my navy pumps and put them up against the wall before testing the carpet. I try the pinkish one first, the one I like least. It reminds me of the color of Carrie's belly. I put both feet on it and think of her crying the night before, like some kind of trapped animal. I look up to clear my head from all of that and I see Louis grinning back at me. "That's gonna feel mighty fine on my toes, when I get up to make your coffee in the morning," he says.

And for the only time since I've met her, I'm glad to see Sarah coming into the room just then so I don't have time to respond. She's nineteen years younger than Louis, a change-of-life baby. I guess their momma and daddy gave up trying, and then she came along, and they were so happy to have her that they spoiled her, so she always expected to be taken care of. Louis was like another daddy to her. When he took her around with him, people thought he was her daddy. Maybe that was how he knew to take care of me and Cedric, because of her. She's two years older than Cedric and still dressing like a teenager. It makes me wonder if young women today have any sense at all.

"Where're the boys?" she says to us without even a hello. She's not trying to be rude, she just doesn't have any manners. Maybe her momma tried; it just didn't take.

"They outside. Which one you like best?" he asks her, and I can't stop myself; I look at him, mouth open. Why in the hell would he be asking her? Louis tries to save himself, saying, "You ladies are better at this kind of thing," like he'd actually meant to ask the both of us. I don't even pretend to care. I slip my shoes on while Sarah touches a finger to her chin with a frown on her face like she's picking out a million-dollar ring, and I walk over to the sliding glass doors, watching the boys trying to hook up a yellow sprinkler to the hose so they can cool off. I can feel the heat through the glass.

"I think this one," she says in that squeaky girl-voice of hers, like she's scared someone might mistake her for a grownup. I take my time before I turn around, and there she is, grinning, perched on the pink square, kneading it with her bare toes like a kitten.

It doesn't make me feel any better that, judging from the look on Louis' face, he doesn't like that one, either. Maybe it looked better in the showroom, but then you get it out in the real light of day, and you see it won't work. I say, "I think that looks cheap." I get my pocketbook strap up over my shoulder—I never even put it down the whole time we were there—and walk out the front door without even a glance at either of them.

I know I've just given Sarah and her momma years of things to talk about, mainly what an uppity bitch I am, and how, seeing what I come from, I ought to behave myself. His momma is nice enough to me but she'd rather Louis be with Karina, where her grandchildren are. But I don't care. The thing propelling me to the door is the idea of that pink carpet covering the floors of this house. I can see Louis letting her pick it out just like he's let her stay long past her welcome. And she's not moving anytime soon; the place is just as stuffed with junk as it always has been since I first saw it.

To his credit, it doesn't take Louis long to get out the door after me. "What's wrong with you, baby?" he says, following me to the car.

"We ready to go yet?"

"Hey, now." He puts his hands on my shoulders to stop me. He turns me to him. "What got into you?"

"Don't you talk to me like I'm some child," I say. "I see what's going on. That woman's never leaving this place."

"What?"

"You see any boxes up in there?"

Louis looks down at me, truly confused, his hands still on my shoulders, and I wonder if I dreamed what he said about her leaving. "That woman is my sister," he says quietly, still with that tone like I've disappointed him, the way my father sounded when I told him I was going to marry Tony.

"That's right," I say, stepping away from his arms. "She's your sister. Not your child. You don't have to let her run you."

Louis looks at the house and then at me, shaking his head. "She don't run me."

"I give it two weeks and that pink shit is going to be all over the place."

He laughs. "Is that what this is all about? A color?"

"If you think that, you done lost your mind. What do you want from me anyway? Talking about making me coffee every morning, but you don't even have a place to live, and all I've got to reach you is a cell phone. You might as well be something I made up. I've felt that way, you know, from the first time you called me."

I look back at the house. Louis left the front door cracked, like he planned to go back in there. Let him do it, I think. I'll start walking. And I don't care what Sarah hears.

"Lullaby," he says, doing what he can to reach me. "I'm real."

"Then tell me this, because it's something I don't know, so I can't make it up."

I've got his attention now. He nods, waiting.

"Why did you call me?"

He takes a step toward me, and I take a step back. I hear the hiss of the sprinkler, the boys shrieking out back. He pulls his keys out of his pocket. "How about we just go."

"What, you don't want to tell me?"

"I don't want to go through this whole thing out in the yard."

"I don't either," I tell him. "But we can't go inside *your* house, can we?"

Louis pinches the top of his nose, right between his eyes. There's sweat above his eyebrows and on his chin. I like that, seeing him trying to think of what to say. "After I broke my back, I started thinking about you."

He's said this kind of thing before, about how having something like that happen to you can change your life. So I'm waiting for more, because I know all about that. Being sliced open and left for dead changes you, too—I could say it, but I don't want those white trash, who for all I know are within a mile of me at this very moment, to have that kind of power over me. I don't even want to breathe them into the air.

Louis says, "When you're laying up in traction you have time to think about every single day you've lived. If you could remember being born I would've done it. And I got to thinking how you used to joke about your trigger finger. You remember that? When you broke your thumb right after Cedric was born?"

"Tony broke it," I say, my voice tight in my throat.

He looks at the ground. "You said, 'As long as my trigger finger's working, I'm okay.' You remember?"

"Yes," I breathe, rather than say. My dress is sticking to my back.

"Well, I kept thinking about that. That's why I called."

I'm back thirty years again, sitting on that porch in the cool of the night with him, so dark we couldn't see each other's faces. The night he first called me Lullaby. Because my eyes looked sleepy, he said. He didn't know they were just swollen, still bruised, caked over with makeup I made from clay and spit. And how I loved him for what he didn't know, sitting close enough to touch on that step, balancing a bottle on his knee, but never so much as touching me, so I could've dreamed him even then.

But the woman I am now is present, too. And she wonders how it took a year between Louis remembering me making fun of my broken bones, and then finally calling me on that rainy night. "You were still trying to get her back," I said, thinking of Karina's smile in the picture he has in his wallet even now, the smile of a woman who knows she's beautiful. "You took me only when you knew what you couldn't have."

Louis touches his mouth with both hands, as if wiping away the first thing he was going to say. He drops his arms to his sides. "Woman, I never took you. I asked for you. Now, I need to know what you want from me. You want me to deny my past life and my family? That's just not possible. You want me to love you, then you have me."

There is nothing left in me except this flash of rage that it wasn't him I saw at church that one Sunday, after I'd been healing from the rape for a year and wasn't limping anymore, that it had to be Tony instead, who I'd known and been scared of all my life. That Louis' family had to choose another church, that our children couldn't be ours together. The rage chokes me, takes my words away, even the blood from my legs, so I have to lean against him when he puts his arm around me and walks me to the car.

It's not fifteen minutes later, Louis is driving us to get lunch, when he starts sneaking a smile at me every few seconds.

"What?"

He says, "You and that carpet. Pink shit. Lord help me."

We laugh all afternoon. We don't worry about the noise, making love in my bedroom in the middle of the day. Later, I ask him which carpet he liked best. "I liked the gray one," he says, and I say, "Me too," and that seems like a good sign.

I call Social Services the next morning. There's a separate number if you think a child is being abused or neglected—what's the difference? I give what I know—her first name, her age, the other people in the apartment. I give the address. I tell about the late-night yelling and banging. "She's out on the street a lot," I tell the flat-voiced woman. "She goes around begging cigarettes and who knows what else." The only thing I don't tell is about the night before, when I heard her crying. Maybe that's because right then I'm thinking of Cedric, and how one morning when I woke up on the floor, my face aching from a beating and from the drink I'd taken to ease the pain, he had curled his two-year-old body into mine and was crying so hard I knew he'd had to have been at it for hours. That child-whine, yes, I know it.

The woman says they'll send someone out but she doesn't say who, or when. It could be weeks. It could be cops or some lone do-gooder with a notebook. The not knowing makes me more nervous than having called in the first place.

I hang up and call Louis on his cell to tell him I did it. He tells me he's going to stop by his house and pick up the carpet samples, which we forgot after our fight and all the making up, and then he's going see his mechanic because there's something wrong sounding in the engine of his Jeep. He says he'll come over after they're finished.

"I'll fix you dinner," I say, and he says okay, and I can hear the smile in his voice. But the next thing I hear after we hang up is people moving around next door. I decide to get out and take the bus over to the mall, and then I ride to the grocery store to pick up a few things. By the time I get back, it's about time to start cooking.

I'm putting away my groceries when there's a knock on the door. I know it can't be Louis because I would've heard the Jeep. I look through the peephole, and it's the girl, holding the screen open with her hip. I stand there, trying to decide. *Calm down*, I tell myself. *Social services can't be running any one-day turn-around.*

She knocks again. She says through the door, "I just want a cigarette."

I open up partway. "I don't have any."

She shifts her weight from one skinny flank to the other. "You just went shopping."

I take in the fact that she's been watching my comings and goings. "You know you shouldn't be smoking with a baby," I say. I wonder what Louis would do right now. Maybe he'd just come right out with it: *Who raped you?*

"This baby ain't going anywhere 'til it's ready," she says. She doesn't smile. She doesn't bop and fidget like most girls. Something in her is dead still.

"You don't know that."

Her eyes flick away from mine. "You never smoked with your babies?"

"One."

"Thanks," she says, thinking I mean I'll give her one.

"No, I mean I had one, a boy," I said. "And yes, I smoked. But that was back before they knew it was bad. You want to keep it?"

"What the hell else am I supposed to do?"

I look at her for a moment. I want to slap her for two reasons. One, because I hate rude kids, especially when they're up in my house begging. And two, if I'd ever talked that way, I sure as shit would have been slapped.

"You could've gotten rid of it."

"My mother won't go for that."

"But she's okay with you messing around?"

"I didn't *mess* around," she says, eyes shiny as glass, chin out, teeth gritted. Her turn to get mad. Fine by me. I didn't ask her to come over.

"Well, all it takes is once," I say. "But I guess you know that now." I reach for my new pack, because I'm ready for her to get gone, but then she starts laughing.

"I wish," she says, when I shake one out and hand it to her. She's laughing so hard her belly jiggles up and down. "I fucking *wish*."

She slams the door behind her, as if she wants to shut out whatever I'd have to say to that. I listen for her back door to open, but it doesn't. After a minute, I lock the back and go out the front. I can smell where she is from the smoke; she's standing with her back against the end of the building, right under my bedroom window. When I come around the corner, she jumps, her shoulders shrugging up. I ask her what her name is. She takes her time answering, trying not to show I scared her. "Carrie."

I say, "That was me, tapping last night."

She drags on the cigarette and blows out again, her face as blank as a wall. I could not even be standing there. "How old is your son?"

"Thirty-three." So now I know, because she's pretended not to hear what I said, that it was her, sitting on the floor with her back to that thin wall, crying.

"He married?"

"No." I want to stop there but I keep going. "He's got two kids though, by two different mothers." I'm not sure what I mean by telling her that. Maybe so she knows she can't trap a man with a baby. I hate to use my son as an example. I love him. But the only person he's ever stuck by is Tony, who's living in Section Eight these days and waiting on his EBT card to roll over each month. I could tell him about how his daddy beat me to the floor and kicked me in the stomach until I passed out when I was five months gone with him. How he left us to starve out there in the woods. But he knows that; he was there. And he also remembers the years I left him with his great-aunt while I went to Atlanta, first to get away from Tony, and then to dry out. He remembers how, when I came back, still shaking, he was ten years old and had no idea who I was.

Carrie stubs her cigarette in the ground. "Well, I'm not getting married," she says.

"Maybe you will."

"No." She lifts her chin, looking up past me, past our building. "Someday I'll live in a tent and go swimming in the ocean every day. That's the way it'll be."

She walks back toward her apartment in no particular hurry. From behind you can't even tell she's pregnant unless you knew to look for that thickness over the hips.

When I get back inside, the phone is ringing. I'm relieved that it's Louis, but then I can tell from the way he's talking fast that something's wrong.

"Wait a minute," I say, turning down the TV. "Start over."

"She didn't pay the taxes. The house is in default."

"Well, just pay them." I think about giving him the money if he needs it, but then I decide that's gonna depend on Sarah getting out. I didn't save all those years working at this and that job just to hand over money to support that girl.

"You're not getting it."

"All right, explain it to me."

He tells me that when he went to get the carpet samples, the mailman had just come, so he decided to take the mail in. Then he saw the notice marked "URGENT" from the county tax department and opened it while waiting for Sarah to come to the door.

"It said they are gonna evaluate the house for auction to pay the past due taxes because the taxes are over a certain percent of the value."

"You just need to go down there and work something out with them," I say as I unwrap the chicken and wash it. I should be sharing in his worry, but right then I'm actually happy. That bitch is going to be gone from that house. *Out of there*, I'm thinking.

"I *went* down there and they wouldn't even talk to me. The person I'm supposed to see ain't in. So now I'm at the garage and the guy's telling me they might need to keep the damn thing overnight."

"You can get in to talk to someone tomorrow, I'm sure. They want their taxes more than they want your house. How you gonna get home?"

He says he doesn't know. His mother doesn't have a car, and of course I don't either. After making it all those years in the woods with no car, I figured I could handle town. "What about Sarah?" I say just as sweet as you please. "She owes you a favor about now."

"I can't get her to save my life. I left her at the house, bawling her eyes out. I've been calling her cell, I've called Momma to see if she's gone over there." He sounds more than nervous; his breathing is funny. "Momma's all upset. She's about to have a stroke."

I sit there and try to think. I keep going back to the taxes. "What did they want you to do? Pay by a certain date?"

"I told you it's past that, long past." His voice sounds strangled. "The letter was talking about a hearing that happened *last week*."

"They can't send you something about a hearing after the fact. Now that's just crazy." I'm about to say that he just needs to leave his car and get someone to bring him on over here, and we'll talk it out. I decide I'll give him the money he needs, whatever he needs, no strings, although I bet he's going to get Miss Sarah out of there so fast it'll make her little head spin. Let her move in with momma for a while, see how she likes it. Might be some birth control for her, even. "Listen," I say, but Louis cuts me off.

"They sent it weeks ago. She just let it sit in the box. Can you *believe* that?"

I decide it won't help to say that yes, I most certainly can. "Louis. Get your car if it'll drive. Come over here. We can take care of this."

He tells me he'll catch a ride with one of the mechanics if his car isn't ready by the end of the day, and I say okay to this, and then I start getting ready. I light candles and put on some smooth jazz. I make a marinade for the chicken and cut up my fattest red tomatoes for a salad, and I remember the nights, years ago, when he brought me food and comforted me when I thought the world had spit me out, and I feel warm in my chest thinking that now I can do the same for him. *We can save each other on this earth*, I want to tell him.

At six, I figure Louis will be here soon; the garage probably doesn't stay open past then. I put on perfume and take a little time with my makeup and push my hair back from my face with two combs. By the time I'm dressed, I can hear some action next door. The older brother must be home because he's blaring his rap music; I don't know why the mother doesn't do something about that. Course, she might like it herself. While I'm in the kitchen putting rolls on a pan, I see Carrie and her mother coming home in their old blue car with the back bumper missing. Her mother is just a taller, wider version of Carrie. The mother gets out and heads straight for the back door, not even a look at Carrie, who is moving slow, holding onto the car door frame before pushing it shut. Her mouth is pinched, her face turned into itself, like she's sleepwalking.

I turn the chicken in its marinade. I wonder if I should go ahead and get it cooking or wait. I turn on the evening news and watch the day's car accidents and crimes while checking the front window every few minutes. By seven, I'm getting irritated. I don't want to call Louis because I believe he should call me—what's wrong with men and phones? Do they just never learn to use them, like how they can't ever seem to write decent?

When I finally call, my stomach's growling and I'm fuming. "Louis, after you calling me all upset you ought to tell me what's going on here. Where are you?" I hang up. Sometimes his cell doesn't ring but then he gets the voicemail because it starts chirping. I give it fifteen minutes and try again. "Louis, I am worried about you. Call me now."

After another hour, with the dark gathering in the trees across the street, I'm so mad I feel like crying. There have been times when he hasn't called me back until the next day, but never when we had plans. Didn't we have plans? Maybe he changed his mind and went home if he had to leave his car at the shop, because there'd be no way for him to get home on the busses from here. Plus, Louis doesn't like busses; he has a little pride about not using them. *Think,* I tell myself. I don't want to call his momma, but finally I do it. She's got that caller ID and usually won't pick up when I call, but this time she does. She hasn't heard from Louis either. I ask if Sarah's talked to him.

"No, she over here now." She sounds upset, and I don't know if she's worried about him or the house taxes.

"Please ask him to call me."

She says she will, and I try his cell again. Nothing but voicemail.

I close the shades and turn on some lights. I gnaw on a roll, but I don't want to give in and eat just yet. The music next door is thumping good now, TV noise humming in the walls. I hoped it would calm down over there with the mother home, but no such luck.

Normally I love this apartment, the only place I've ever had to myself, but right now I feel trapped in it. Still, even if I could get in a car I wouldn't know where to start looking. I don't know where the garage is. I don't know where Louis spends his time when he's not with me. I'm too old to go asking after a man's every move.

But tonight I wish I did know. I'm crying by the time I put that chicken into a baking dish and set the timer.

At midnight I finally make myself get ready for bed. I put the chicken right in the fridge. I hang up my clothes and wipe off my makeup. I've already cleaned the kitchen and called Louis so many times his voicemail won't take any more messages.

I sit in bed with the lamp on, looking at a magazine, knowing I won't sleep, not only because of Louis but also because of that damned music. It's been a long time since I felt helpless. My worry is like a rock in the pit of my hips. Already, someone yelling next door—I can hear it all the way on the other end of the apartment with my bedroom door closed. They might as well go crazy over there, I think, since I can't sleep anyway. I get out of bed and change out of my nightgown into a pair of leggings and a T-shirt. In the living room I flip through the channels in the dark.

Eventually, I do fall asleep: I don't know when. Then my eyelids pop open right in the middle of a dream, my ears cocked, like they did when I would sit up listening for Tony. You never forget it, that kind of waiting. It's quiet except for my TV, which I click off with the remote. I sit up on the couch. Some sound woke me up; I can remember it now that I'm awake. It was something being dropped hard on the floor. The floor still seems to be shivering from it, and the quiet has changed, heavy like the air right before thunder.

Another slam, and a scream, and I scream, too, because it's the kind of cry that tears your own voice out of your throat. I'm on my feet, hunting for the phone, which I thought I'd left on the coffee table but can't find in the dark, and I'm sure not going to turn on any lights. I stuff my hands between the couch cushions, thinking it might have slipped underneath. Another slam, this time against my wall, and more screaming, and I know it's Carrie, and I know someone is beating the living hell out of her.

I run to the kitchen window, pull back the curtain as wide as my eye, and look out into the parking lot. The mother's car isn't there. Carrie's screaming has a rhythm to it now—a couple of bursts and then a shriek that seems to keep going even after she stops. I can hear her running, the pounding in my floorboards. And I can hear a man's voice, which, if you weren't used to these things, you'd think was the talk of someone who's under control. But he's not trying to calm her down. Tony used to get real quiet like that when he was hitting me. He'd hit me and then say a few things about why I deserved it while he rested his arm. But there was something stretched tight in his voice—it makes me shake to remember it now—like a wire about to break.

I rip the cushions off the couch, and there's the phone. I call 911 first. Then, even though I know he won't answer by now, I call Louis just to hear his voice before the fake woman's voice says, "Mail box 6295 is full. Please try again later." I take the phone with me into the bedroom and take my gun out of my bedside table and sit down on my bed and load it, right there in the dark. I took a class. I don't need to see to be able to do it.

Sit tight, sit tight, I say to myself, the gun putting its own dent in the mattress beside me. I never thought I'd be hugging myself in the dark, terrified, ever again. I listen to Carrie screaming and that terrible low voice and shit flying around all over the place next door. *Stay alive,* I say to her.

And right then their front door flies open so hard that the storm door hits the side of the building. The sound of breaking glass. The screaming trails like something burning all the way outside. I figure she's running down the street, and I make myself stand up, part the blind, and look out my bedroom window to see which way she goes, so I can tell the cops. I get a fix on her just as the man tackles her in the yard near the curb. I can't tell who it is, but I'm guessing it's the mother's boyfriend, or it's just some random man. Just some trash who thinks he can do whatever he wants to a woman.

I don't remember getting myself from that bed to my front stoop. I'm just all of a sudden standing out there, pointing the gun. I know I've said something, because I can feel my voice rub in my throat, but I don't know what words make the man look up at me. By then I'm too busy trying to watch his hands, because a gun can flutter like a bird to a man's fingertips; I've seen it. He's sitting on her hip, and she's twisted onto her side, arms over her belly until she hears me, too. Then she lifts her arms and squints where I stand in porch light, and I see the inky blood working its way down her neck, and I wish I'd thought to turn off that porch light because I am a target up here.

The man moves and I look back in his eyes, and I see then that he's her brother, and I know he's the one who raped her, because there can be no other explanation for this. His eyes are pale and narrow, and he is getting up.

"Give me a reason," I tell him. I want to cry. He stands there in his baggy ghetto pants and sports jersey, brushing his straw-colored hair out his eyes. Between his ankles, his sister sobs. Maybe she's been crying the whole time; maybe I'm just now hearing her.

"Fuck off, bitch," he says, and since I've already cocked the gun, I just raise it an inch and take aim for the center of the zero on his chest. He steps off of her. Behind him the trees are flickering red and blue from the lights coming around the corner off Church Street. She's on her hands and knees, crawling, and Brother and I are looking deep in each other's eyes, steady as lovers. The last time a white man said bitch to me I was on my stomach, face in the gravel. But now I'm on my feet. I am as still as the air.

There's two cop cars and an ambulance right behind them. As soon as they come out of their cars I'm setting down the gun. It doesn't surprise me at all that one of their guns is pointing straight at me. I come down the steps slow and let one pat me down while another runs in my front door. I don't know how many of them there are. Brother's up against the other car, his face as dull as a club. There's blood on his knuckles, on his neck.

Carrie's on her back on a gurney, EMTs on either side. When I come over, she looks in my direction. "I told my mother," she says then, her voice thick. Her hips are so small she makes the gurney look wide. Her face is a mask of blood; her nose is folded to one side, her left eye is swelling shut. She looks older than I ever thought I'd live to be.

I want to say goodbye to her. But I can't, my jaws are shaking too hard. I watch the ambulance pull away and hope my voice comes back in time for me to give my statement.

As dawn comes, I am thankful that all the liquor stores are closed and the grocery stores can't sell any wine or beer yet. I want a drink so bad my throat burns for it. I used to have to put my forehead to the floor when it was really bad. Nothing else worked. All through the morning I drink glass after glass of water and crouch next to my bed, rubbing my forehead on the rug. I can't go to sleep for all my crying and peeing.

When the phone wakes me up, I'm still on the floor, and I can look up and see the sun-white sky through the slits of my closed blinds. I pull the phone off the bed and fumble to answer it. "Louis," I say, knowing it's him. Or wanting it enough to know.

He tells me where he is, but the words don't make sense. "What?"

"I'm in jail."

Somehow I get confused, and I think he's in jail because of what happened here last night. I open the blind and see the heat pulling off the street. But then he's asking me to pick him up, something about where to post the bond. He asks me if I can borrow the neighbor's car.

"No, I can't borrow any car from those people. I'll take a cab."

The bondsman is downtown right across the street from the county jail, which is a box the color of wet concrete. In the cells on the upper floors, there are slits for windows. The idea that my Louis and that little shit from next door could be locked in the same building makes me want to throw up.

I tell the cabbie to wait. He's white but he can hardly say anything in English. "Wait," I say again, and he nods. I pay the bond, then cross the street. The cabbie watches me through his dirty windshield, and I figure he's seen a thousand of me, some woman coming to claim her man like a lost dog.

A bald deputy leads me to a room. I sit in a plastic chair and wait for half an hour. Finally, the same deputy comes back with Louis in front of him. He takes off Louis' cuffs and tells him to take care. He tells us where the exit is. We pick up Louis' things at the window from another deputy, a white woman with an underbite so bad she spits with every word. Before we walk about the door, he tucks his button-down striped shirt into his dark jeans and threads his belt through the loops. He's walking off balance; his back's hurting.

I'm glad to see the cab still idling at the curb. "What the hell happened?" I ask.

"Just wait," he says as we get in. He stares out the window all the way home.

When we get into my apartment, I wonder if he can sense the hitting and the blood in the air like the perfume I dabbed on the night before, expecting him. When I put coffee on, I see out the window that Carrie's mother's car is gone, and I wonder where she went first, the hospital or the jail.

Louis sits heavily in the chair against the wall at my kitchen table. I get out cold chicken from last night and slice it for sandwiches. I haven't eaten anything all day and I'm shaking from it, from everything. When I bring him a glass of water, he says, "That son of a bitch wouldn't let me get my car."

I sit down across from him.

"They were done with it. But the owner'd gone, and the guy wouldn't let me pay up and go. Said the register was closed. And— I was like, '*Look*, man,' but he wouldn't do anything except stand there shaking his head." He sucks in his breath and looks down at his arms resting on the table. "And so I just hit him. I knocked him down and got my keys off the board and he grabbed the phone and called the cops." Louis looks at me, and there's something flat behind those dark eyes. "And I ain't running from no one, now."

"Louis, what did you think—?"

"I didn't think they'd arrest me."

Normally I'd ask him if his brain got crushed under that wall along with his back. A white guy hits someone and it's a dispute; a black guy does the same thing and it's an attack. He rests his forehead on his fists. "That goddamned house."

"That house doesn't control you," I say, and I make myself stop there. Then I tell him about Carrie, and I ease myself closer to him so our heads are almost touching, and I stay quiet when he squeezes me to him and doesn't let go.

Later, I want to tell him, we'll find out how he can keep his house. After that, we'll move in, and his girls will visit in summer, and we'll get ready for our old age and deaths together. Before I leave this place, Carrie will have her baby and start the school year late with a foster family in another town. I'll never see her again. Her mother and brother will move out and disappear. Brother will do no time.

I touch Louis' face. I'm thinking of the courthouse, all that's left to be done. "We got the day ahead of us," I say. I put a plate with a sandwich in front of him. "Let's go on, now. Let's just go on."

Five-Minute Man

WHEN CHARLIE WAS SEVEN, his mother Lola was convinced he'd be famous because he'd won a starring role in an M&M's commercial. They flew from Tampa to New York, Lola preparing him all the way for the stardom that would follow. "Walk slowly, because people don't respect anyone in a rush," she said, and, "Take a lady's hand, don't shake it." In the commercial, he popped a red M&M past his Vaseline-smeared teeth and then, smiling brightly, showed his clean, open palm as the jingle sang "Melts in your mouth, not in your hand!" This was in the seventies, before everyone started saying the red dye caused cancer. Anyway, he did this perfectly the first time, and the producer, a short, balding man, squeezed his shoulders and put his red face close to Charlie's and said, "Son, you are gonna take off like a rocket."

Charlie wondered, as he tied on his yellow Camera Town apron with brown piping and an appliqué of a single lens reflex camera, whether at thirty-one he could still be considered a late bloomer. The aprons were new. The owner's wife had sewn the camera on too low, so the camera hovered just above his crotch, which made him self-conscious. Sometimes customers glanced at it and then looked away slightly embarrassed, and he wanted to explain that this had not been his idea, and he hoped that they had not been made to feel uncomfortable. In general, he felt apologetic.

Under the apron Charlie wore jeans and a T-shirt that said

"Cleveland Rock and Roll Hall of Fame" on the back, which his sister Rose sent him after breaking up with her last boyfriend, a tone-deaf bass player who'd gotten audited for trying to write off his season pass as professional research. Charlie tried tucking in the T-shirt and then tucking the apron into the waistband of his jeans a little ways so that the camera moved farther up his abdomen, but it kept slipping out again. He looked at his co-worker Rich, who smirked somewhat unsympathetically over the shoulder of a customer inspecting a used Leica. Rich was a student at Manatee Community College in Sarasota, where Charlie had begun a short career over ten years ago. He'd declared three majors in his time there: journalism, because he wanted to be an investigative reporter; theater, because his mother kept reminding him of his excellent profile and the fame he need only pluck from his future like a bright Florida orange; and finally photography, which led him to the job at Camera Town, where he thought he could get some practical experience for the summer. But then he'd decided to stop school and work for a year to get his bearings, and that turned into years, and since then he'd sold a lot of used single lens reflex cameras to Photography 101 students.

The heat had come early this season. The afternoon air settled wetly on Charlie's skin and the sun burned through the thinning muslin-colored hair at his crown as he left for the day and got into his 1989 white Toyota Corolla with the itchy maroon interior and the bumper sticker on the back window that said "Got Jesus?" His mother Lola had added it before giving the car to him, having turned briefly to religion following a hit-and-run accident that had not injured her but had nearly totaled the car. The corner was shredded where he'd tried to remove it, but Lola had caught him at it on one of her many drop-ins, and became concerned for his soul, and suggested that, at the very least, removing it might be bad luck, so he'd let it stay. He backed out carefully and pulled onto Midnight Pass Road, heading home. The car's alignment had never been completely restored, so it listed curbward like a bent shopping cart.

Charlie knew Lola's concerns were motivated by a perhaps overlarge love for him, since his father had left years ago, and she only had two friends, Norma and Nina, elderly sisters who lived in a 1950's neighborhood on the other side of Tamiami Trail, whose names he had never, after all these years, been able to keep straight. They both had short gray hair and wore matching outfits a lot of the time even though they weren't twins. While he was often irritated by the cutesey similarity of their names and attire, at that moment he regretted that he hadn't ever figured out a way to remember which was Norma and which was Nina. He drove slowly behind a shell-pink Mercedes, twisting the steering wheel slightly left to continue straight, and he could actually feel the regret spread in his chest like a bruise. These moments always led him to a string of unpleasant questions, like why he'd dropped out of college, and whether he should've pursued an acting career, and what would happen if a truck hit him hard enough to knock his car into Tampa Bay, as had nearly happened to his mother.

He pulled into the Sunset Beach apartment complex, where he'd been living for six years now after moving out of his mother's house, and rounded the corner to the parking space he always used at the base of the stairs nearest to his second-floor apartment, but there was a moving van parked parallel to the building, which blocked about six spaces. This irritated him, and then he felt guilty for being irritated because, after all, moving is stressful, and by the time he'd parked his car across the lot, he felt completely defeated. As the air heated around him, he let his head fall back against the seat and contemplated his evening: microwaved pizza and ESPN until he fell asleep on the couch his mother had given him when he moved. He was wiping at the sheen of sweat on his face, eyes closed, when there was a knock so hard on his window he thought a rock had fallen on it.

"Hello?" A large blond woman with close-together eyes and a wide mouth was looking down at him in a pleading way, as if her foot were trapped under his wheel.

He sat up in the seat, embarrassed to be caught like that, mouth open, the sweaty white crease of skin in the middle of his throat fully visible. He fumbled for the door handle, then decided to roll down the window. "Sorry," he said, not sure what he meant by it except that he wanted her to know he wasn't a private detective or a pervert.

"Oh, it's okay," she said, the automatic response. "Actually, I was wondering if you could help me lift something. I'm sorry to ask."

"No, no, that's fine, I mean, don't be sorry." He opened the door too fast and bumped her with it; she stepped back and smiled, shaking her head as he apologized again. He guessed from the crinkles around her eyes that she was older than he, but the roundness of her face made her look young. She wore a lot of makeup like Lola, with an orange tinge that lined her jaw and seemed to be melting on her forehead, chin, and cheeks right under the eyes, where she was sweating. She was almost as tall as he, which was five-eleven, though he said six even. And she was big all over—thick arms and legs, a shelf of breasts, broad shoulders.

"It's my file cabinet," she said. "My kids could help me with everything but that."

Right then the kids burst screaming out of the apartment next door to his, which had been blissfully quiet and empty for two months after his neighbor Ruby had moved to an assisted living facility. Ruby had been quite deaf and had done all the things people who cling to the illusion that their senses remain intact are prone to do, such as scream into the telephone while the TV blared. Charlie watched the kids thumping down the stairs, two boys and a girl, and sighed. Their mother patted his shoulder. "They're good kids," she said. "I promise we won't bother you."

The kids stomped down the stairs to the parking lot, sounding like one large, many-legged, hurried animal. The two younger ones threw themselves at their mother, finding purchase on one ample hip each; the older boy stood a few feet away. Trying out his man-stare. "Hi," Charlie said to them.

The woman didn't wait for the response that wasn't going to come. "I'm Melanie and this is Kyle," she said, pointing to the older boy. Then, her hands touching the heads of the other two, "Troy and Ann Marie." Troy looked to be about eight and Ann Marie about five or six, Charlie wasn't sure; he wasn't good with kids' ages. He knew what he'd looked like at seven on the TV screen, arms brown and thin and face shiny with the pleasure of doing well. The rest had faded.

"Pleased to meet you. Charlie," he said to them all. Always in a dark chocolatey corner of his heart he thought of what could have been if his acting career had flared from that commercial, people eager to shake his hand rather than looking away from him, attention fading. Melanie had started walking toward the moving van, and he followed.

"This is it," she said. The black four-drawer file cabinet, looking monolithic and weighty as a building, was the last item in the van save a couple of boxes. Kyle jumped into the van and grabbed one of them. As he jumped out again, hugging the box, he sneered at Charlie, one corner of his mouth drawn up, as if to make a point: *bet you can't do that.*

Charlie stared back at Kyle, imagining, he had to admit to himself, smacking the child open-handed as his father had once done not long after the commercial and before he'd left for good, calling him sullen.

"I've got a dolly, but it's too heavy for me to manage alone," Melanie said.

He couldn't miss the sound of her voice, even in the midst of his brief fantasy of decking her child. The tone was sweet without being too girlish, full and warm with the slightest ring. She sounded like a grown woman, but a beautiful, rich one, not a divorced, overweight and probably financially strapped one, based on her choice of these apartments. He turned to her. She smiled, and he thought she knew about this voice of hers. Just like another woman might know her eyes are her best feature, or her legs, or her hair.

"How about I pull it up the stairs, and you push," Charlie said.

It was no joke getting the thing to the second-floor breezeway. The kids played near the open door, trying to slide on the doormat, and it made him nervous the whole way up; the vibrations from their antics made him feel he'd lose hold of the thing, crush this woman. She grunted quietly at each push, but even her grunts sounded great. In truth, the sound of her huffing and puffing turned him on, which was probably related to the fact that he hadn't been with a woman in, well, call it five years, and that had been a near accident, really; the woman thought he was someone she knew. She'd made that clear. "I thought you were the piano player at the circus," she'd said, still sitting on him afterward, drunk, laughing at her mistake.

Once Charlie and Melanie hauled the cabinet on the straining dolly over the last step and got to the doorway, the kids held the door open as they passed. She led him to the smallest bedroom in the back corner. Except for the fact that this was a three-bedroom apartment and his was one-bedroom, it looked exactly the same—gray carpet worn in the traffic areas, chalk-white walls. Small kitchen with breakfast bar and living dining area in front. It just went further back to accommodate the two extra bedrooms. He'd been in it before, to help Ruby carry things, and every room had been packed with antiques, stacked newspapers and wall-hangings. Empty, it somehow looked smaller.

"Well," Charlie said when he'd leaned the tall cabinet off the dolly and managed to turn it around against the wall where she'd indicated.

"Thanks very much," she said, still breathing heavily in a not unattractive way.

"No problem." He wanted to know what was in the thing. Every drawer was locked. "So, is this for your work?"

"Yes," she said. "I'm lucky. I get to work from home, so I'm there for my kids when they get home."

"That's nice. Wish I could work from home," he said. But

actually, the idea of never having a reason to leave his apartment scared him—how would he be different from Ruby then? He followed Melanie out into the living room, where the kids were milling around, looking at the boxes and garbage bags spilling towels and clothes, not sure what to get into first. They had either packed in a hurry or this was just the way she packed. He didn't have a good feel for moving an entire family; except for his couch and bed, he'd moved everything he'd needed from his mother's house in two carloads. "How'd you manage that, anyway?"

"What?" she said.

"Working from home."

"Oh, I do web sites."

"Oh," Charlie said. He'd seen the computer on the floor in the smallest bedroom that he figured would be her office with all the wires and such. He hadn't explored the Internet very much except for some brief forays into porn sites, just to see if it were true that you could actually view that stuff without going to a convenience store and having to ask for the magazine from some skinny kid who probably felt sorry for you because he was getting the real thing and you weren't, then carrying the thing out to your car, brown wrapper like a flag for porn, and into your apartment, which he'd only done a couple of times. He didn't have a computer; they still had a cash register at work where you punched in the numbers, no scanners or what not. His sister kept wanting to e-mail him things and he had to remind her he didn't use e-mail, so sometimes she printed out the latest funny chain email she'd gotten or sick warnings, like people getting their hamstrings cut by someone lurking under cars in mall parking lots, and mailed it to him with notes about joining the twenty-first century.

"Thanks again," Melanie said then. "When we get settled, I'd like to have you over for dinner."

"Oh, you don't have to—"

"I'll knock on your door sometime."

"Ok," he said, amazed again at the gentle richness of her voice.

It was creamy; he could hear it even after she shut the door, and he didn't even turn on the TV for several minutes once he got into his apartment until he could no longer recreate it in his head.

CAMERA TOWN WAS THE ONLY developer in Sarasota that would process pornographic photographs. Not the professional kind, but the kind people took of their girlfriends or wives. The chains wouldn't develop them; they just returned the negatives with a note about store policy. But Camera Town, as the owner Stu often reminded Charlie and Rick, was an independently-owned establishment, and had to do something to stay ahead of the big boys. Plus, Stu liked to look at the "nudies," as he called them. If some of the shots came out wrong—too much contrast ("hot" being the development term), or too cool—he kept the rejects. Charlie estimated that Stu had pictures of half the women in town and a lot of tourists, too, all of them marred in some way— smudged with the orange glare of a light-damaged negative, or too pale so their noses disappeared and their nipples were the only part of their breasts you could see. Or too dark, so the details receded into shadow. The days when Charlie worked the Fuji developer, he tried to click through the shots as quickly as possible, and he shredded the rejects while Stu wasn't looking. He'd not seen any worth keeping, anyway; most of the women were overweight or starting to sag in places. Not all of them, though. One guy brought in a roll of shots taken in a dorm room, and he'd shot his subject only from the neck down, maybe as a courtesy to her, but probably also because that's all he was interested in anyway. She had a beautiful body, slim thighs and perfectly round breasts with upturned nipples. Still, those headless shots looked a little scary, like a crime scene about to happen. And he couldn't ignore that she was real. With magazines he could pretend those women didn't really exist at all; they were just perfectly drawn cartoons, so anything he thought about them while masturbating in the shower was okay—he wasn't thinking of someone's girlfriend; or worse, their daughter, or sister. At least they'd been paid.

"How's the camera hanging, hmm?" Rick said to Charlie. They were downstairs behind the counter, filing developed film packets for pick up. Charlie had just wiped down the glass-topped counters along each side of the store which displayed used and new single-lens reflexes, video cameras, point-and-shoots. There were lenses and peripherals behind the counters, film behind the cash register, photo paper, sheets and other supplies on two rows of shelves in the middle. Stu's office was in back—basically a table next to where they broke down boxes from shipments and where he sat with the salesmen who came in with their thick product notebooks. The salesmen loved Charlie. They offered to buy him lunches; Charlie wondered if they thought he was Stu's son.

Rick and Charlie each had on their aprons, but Rick was taller than Charlie so the camera appliqué didn't hover quite as low on his abdomen. Rick thought it was funny; he made jokes about it when his fellow students came in for paper or film. Charlie just felt humiliated—having to wear an apron at all was bad enough, but this, too. "We should just get rid of them—you know?" Charlie said. "Put them out back on garbage day."

"Oh, yeah; that'd show 'em, wouldn't it, big guy?" Rick said as he bounded back upstairs to get the next box of packets to file. The sad part was, Charlie had thought for a moment that Rick was serious, really excited about the idea, a prank they could pull off together (and what would Stu do? Fire them both after how good an employee Charlie had always been?) until he got to the "big guy" part. Then he realized Rick was making fun of him, not necessarily in a mean way, but he could tell that Rick, just like the probably two-dozen guys like him who'd passed through in the last eleven years, saw him for what he was, or at least what he'd decided he was, which was stuck and sad. Back in his early twenties, being stuck was cool, maybe even a little romantic and mysterious, because he wasn't just being a good kid and getting his degree like his mommy and daddy wanted; he was trying to figure out what *he* wanted, what *drove* him, and since he was working full time and living at home, he had a lot of extra money, and his mother had taught him that when you ask a woman out, you pay. And back then he still had all his hair, less gut and therefore a good profile. Of course it was a drag that he was living at home, but he explained that his mother was distraught from his father leaving, and he planned to move out any day. This created a sympathy factor that really couldn't be beat. He fudged a bit on the timing of his father's departure, saying it had been "pretty recent" rather than more like fifteen years.

Stu's wife, a small, quiet woman with pale hair the same color as her skin, came back from lunch and gave Charlie a timid smile as she went back to her office, which had once been a storage closet. She'd started doing the books after retiring from her teaching job. She worked at a desk they'd squeezed in there, and never came out except to go to the bathroom in the back. Charlie had never seen her upstairs in the developing room. Not once in all the years he'd been there. He wondered if she knew about Stu's photo collection. He figured no one knew about his own photos, for which he developed contact sheets while Stu was at lunch. He did his own printing in a rented darkroom at school.

Charlie used a Pentax K1000 from his photography major days, nothing fancy. He took shots around town and on the beach, usually as candid as possible, using a telephoto. He'd heard about photographers getting discovered, one guy for his shots of the passengers on public busses, and some New York cabbie for cityscapes shot out his window while hauling fares. He imagined the photographers themselves in the grainy black-and-white film they favored, and their faces were serious, hollow-cheeked, sad-eyed, as if their subjects had shot into them through their lenses and not the other way around. Charlie couldn't match up to this. He had the sad part down, that was pretty certain, but he was too round-faced and fair to pull off the city darkness that got those other guys into white-walled galleries with people milling around in black, possibly to create negative space, drinking cheap wine and bidding on the latest hard, incisive glimpse of humanity.

His photos were all in color. He looked for shots that swirled in it, the brighter the better. He shot old women in turquoise flip-flops and red muumuus feeling up mangoes at Henson's market, which had been at the base of the bridge leading off the Key for as long as he could remember. He shot kids in their bathing suits and too-big hats building sand castles with bright plastic tools you could get at Henson's, too—a yellow shovel, blue bucket, red rake, a couple of green forms to mold patterns in the wet sand, all caught up in a white mesh basket and selling for $4.99. He liked the Hispanic kids best, whose families came mostly in the summer during the off season, because their skin glowed coppery against their bright towels and suits. He shot just-gutted salmon at the fish house down the road, the flesh pink and shiny against the dark scales and blood-stained ice it came packed in off the boats. When he developed the pictures, he wanted to spread the color over himself the way he'd smeared the glowing innards of lightening bugs on his arms one summer at boy scout camp in Georgia because the other kids were doing it; except when he thought of that he now felt a guilty ache, a tenderness in the gut. He wanted to be lifted by that color, filled with it like a cartoon in a fresh coloring book, transformed.

And yes, he liked to shoot women, too, but he was picky. Sometimes the mothers of children he found on the beach. Sometimes groups of girls. Behind the camera he could appraise them, could decide if they were worth the shot, whereas if he'd somehow figured out a way to strike up a conversation with them, he would feel desperate, not sure how to keep their attention, dimly aware of not wanting to appear desperate but unable to stop the eventual glances women shared with each other when signaling a retreat. He'd seen similar stuff on the Nature Channel, when zebras or giraffes eye-balled each other upon sniffing a hyena, whose advance the quiet voice of the announcer calmly described. Except women generally didn't see him as a hyena to be feared, he was pretty sure; it was more along the lines of pity, dismissal. *The female gazelles cut a wide swath around the dying rhinoceros.* But the women he photographed didn't have the opportunity to react to him in this way; most never even saw him. And they were all different. Most guys he knew were attracted to one feature in women, typically the size or shape of breasts or asses. Charlie liked both, to be sure, but it was something in the whole line of the woman that had to catch his eye. He tried to find a pattern, looking through the women in his shots, but they were short and tall; fair and dark, long-haired and short-haired, petite and heavy. Perhaps it was in the way they held themselves, call it grace, or certainty.

Showing these shots to anyone he knew was out of the question. Stu and Rick would probably make fun of him, particularly for the shots of the women. He'd thought about showing them to his sister, but she didn't come home often, usually not unless she was in desperate need of money. He really thought a woman would be the better judge of them. There were a few female professional photographers who had their film developed there—Stu made fun of them as soon as he saw them pull up in their minivans. "Wedding and portrait photography—the girl's sport," he'd say. But when they came in he talked with the seriousness of a psychologist with them about how they wanted their shots developed. The women knew their stuff, but it didn't matter. They would never have respect in Camera Town, with their sisters stacked next to Stu's light table, spreading their legs and smiling for free—and that's the thing about a photograph, Charlie wanted to tell those women, your smile is just as good for us as it is for your lover. The camera makes no distinction.

THAT EVENING, Melanie knocked on his door. She was wearing a tank top and shorts and Charlie couldn't help looking at the fat on her upper arms that gathered in folds at her armpits, the line of her brassiere creating its own bulges at her cleavage and shoulders.

Her hair was wet from the shower, slicked back in a skinny ponytail. She seemed unconcerned about how she looked. *Let herself go*, he could hear his mother saying, his mother who put on what she called her full suit of armor just to go to the grocery store. "Hungry?" Melanie asked in her rich contralto voice.

If only you could photograph sound, Charlie thought. "Uh, I was just going to heat up some pizza."

"Well, I've got baked chicken and rice and a fresh salad just about ready, plenty to spare," she said. "Beer, too."

This all sounded good to Charlie, even if it meant eating with her three kids, whom he could hear in fits of shouts and shrill screams from the youngest, he guessed. In less than a week he'd gotten to where he recognized their voices, which started in the early morning and greeted him when he came home from work, since they'd already gotten home from school, dropped off by the bus that stopped at the end of their row. He didn't want to appear to be giving in on the mention of the beer. "Can I pick up anything?" he asked.

"I think we're set. Just come on when you're ready. The kids are setting the table." She smiled and turned away, leaving him standing at his open door, still listening to her voice as she walked inside her apartment and ordered the kids to pour their drinks. There was a storm coming in off the ocean; he could smell the extra brine in the air mixed with tar in waves of heat rising off the parking lot, and of course there was the watery green cast to the sky. It would be great light for shooting, the beach and surf deep with color, the wind lifting people's hair and making them turn their faces to the sky in a way that looked so noble and contemplative on film. But he was hungry. He touched the soft paunch of his belly and slipped on his Tevas.

Moody Kyle moved over grudgingly to make room for Charlie when Melanie rolled in the chair from her office to the table. The table was pushed against the wall because there wasn't enough room to pull it out and fit chairs around it. Troy and Ann Marie sat on one long side, Kyle and Charlie at the other, with Melanie at the narrow end, her elbows balanced on either side of her plate. She clasped her hands. "Kyle, please say the grace," she said.

Kyle mumbled through "God is great, God is good," while Charlie stared at his plate, hands clasped in his lap. It was as much defiance as he ever had been able muster on those occasions when Lola dragged him along with her and Norma and Nina to Sollie's, where the waiters shouted tunes from the Roaring Twenties at you while you ate over-salted cafeteria food. Before they ate, Lola often held forth with long prayers that were really more like testimonials of her forbearance in the face of ongoing loneliness and lack of clean entertainment for a woman of her age. Even Norma and Nina got twitchy, their bony fingertips tapping the silverware. Charlie looked at his white hands and thought about escape. It wasn't as much a prayer as a mantra. After dinner, they often stayed for the magic show which ran once every hour, and Nina and Norma seemed to be freshly surprised at the same tricks, giggling as they flirted with the fifty-something magician pulling brightly-colored rags from his mouth.

When Kyle finished, Charlie dug into his chicken and rice, wanting suddenly to eat and get out of there. He thought maybe he could make it out to the beach before the storm hit, catch it at its most ripe before letting loose. He could hear the breeze picking up outside. Melanie stood up and brought two more beers from the fridge. Charlie hesitated when she held one up in offer, but she said, "Aw, come on," and opened both and set one by his plate. She took a long drink from hers. "So Charlie, are you from Sarasota?"

Here we go, Charlie thought. This is where I try to gloss over the college dropout episode, the register job. It was better not to try at all. "Actually, I am," he said, leaving it at that.

Melanie was surprised. "Not only is almost no one here under forty, most people aren't from here."

"Yep, my mom is, too—I mean from here. Not under forty."

Melanie smiled. "We're from Miami. But it just got too expensive and I've got family here, too, so we decided to move. We were renting a house on Pineview but the owner put it up for sale and you know how out of sight real estate is around here, too. So, anyway..." her voice trailed off and Charlie felt sorry for her, which was a welcome change from his usual habit of feeling sorry for himself.

"So the Web site business isn't going too good?" he asked. He'd heard people were making a lot of money doing that; his sister had been nagging him about taking some programming courses. *You need to get away from those photo freaks. You could be making 40K in a year*, she'd say to him, sounding like one of those late-night commercials on the local cable access touting pyramid sales schemes. She knew about Stu's photos and the suggestive aprons.

His question seemed to startle Melanie, though. She looked up from her chicken as if he'd called her a name. "Oh, I forgot I told you." Then she relaxed. "Yeah, business is kinda slow. Hasn't helped that we've moved. I need to get more clients around here." She sipped her beer. "So where do you work, anyway? Do they need a Web site?"

"I work at a camera store. I don't think they need a Web site, though."

"Oh," Melanie said. She seemed disappointed.

"So you sell cameras?" Kyle asked in that demanding way of his, as if you owed him an answer to his question.

"Yep, that's pretty much what happens at a camera store. You sell cameras," Charlie said, not able to stop himself from being sarcastic. He could feel Melanie looking at him but he didn't meet her eyes. "And we develop film, tourist shots and the usual, but also all the professional photographers in town come to us," he said, trying to soften his previous comment.

Kyle looked at him, unimpressed. It pissed Charlie off, mostly because he actually wanted the kid to be impressed. "We also develop mug shots for the Sarasota Police Department," he said. That worked.

"No way!" Kyle squealed, unable to contain himself.

"Really?" Troy said. Ann Marie looked excited, too, but she didn't seem to know what they were talking about; she was just trying to follow along.

"What are they like?" Kyle said. "Are people all bloody and stuff?"

Melanie tapped the table to get his attention and flicked her eyes to Ann Marie, whose face had crumpled in concern. "They're bad guys," Melanie said to her. "And the good guys have caught them, and sometimes they fight and get hurt."

"That's bad," Ann Marie said.

Charlie nodded. "Yeah, it is," he said. "Sometimes they are a bit beat up," he said to Kyle. "I'll tell you about it another time, okay?"

"OK." Kyle had gone back to his sullen face, but Charlie felt as if he'd been elected president of something. He'd won the kid over after all.

When they finished, Charlie helped Melanie take out the plates. "We're going out to hunt lightning!" Troy yelled as he and Kyle ran out the door.

Melanie followed. "I want to be able to look out this door and see you. You keep this door in sight. If I don't see you, I'm coming after you and it won't be pretty."

Charlie heard whining noises from the stairs, but Melanie seemed satisfied. She came back in just as Ann Marie turned on the television. "You can watch for one hour, sweetie, and then it's time for bath and bed."

Ann Marie nodded without looking away from the screen where dancing cartoons sang in high-pitched voices. Melanie put the plates in the dishwasher. "Can I help?" Charlie asked, though he didn't want to. He hated cleaning the kitchen more than anything, which why he only ate prepared meals—that and the fact that he couldn't cook.

"This place is so little it doesn't take any time. You ready for another beer?" Melanie asked, opening the fridge. She didn't seem to be in any hurry for him to leave.

"Sure," Charlie said. The second beer had taken the edge off things, and he could just enjoy the moment: the tinny TV songs riding on a rising outside wind, the light gray-green and thick. When Melanie handed him the beer, she checked the boys from the door again and came back to sit at the breakfast bar. "Have a seat if you like," she said. She seemed to wilt a little on the stool, her belly crumpling to three large rolls. Charlie sat, but with his back straight, conscious of his own belly. "Well, I'm impressed," he said, drawing on one of his mother's saner stardom-preparation recommendations, which included giving compliments if you couldn't think of anything else to say. "You got a lot on your plate, with three kids and a job."

"Yeah. My ex pitches in, too," she says. "Totally couldn't make it without that check. He's not a bad guy," she said, smiling a little, as if she realized she was apologizing for him. "Just cheated too much. Kyle caught him in our bed with some piece of ass, and I think he still feels guilty. He should, at least."

Charlie nodded, but the phrase "piece of ass" rang in his ears, especially in her rich voice, and with her daughter in earshot. He stared at his beer to hide his embarrassment. Failed was the term his mother liked to use to describe her own marriage to his father, when she was feeling especially depressed, blaming herself for his father's escape. At times like that he could barely comfort her, because he had to admit he held her partly responsible too, for her insistence on everything being a certain way—the placement of furniture in the room, silverware on the table, people in their lives. There were worse things than being a control freak, he wanted to tell her, but not many were sadder.

"So what about you?" Melanie was asking. "Are you divorced?"

He was actually flattered that someone would assume he was marriageable in the first place. "No, not married yet."

"Anyone special?"

Charlie hesitated.

"Come on, you can tell me. I pick up on people's stories real quick. Anyway, you can rest assured I'm not on the market," she said. "It's going to be a while before I ask these kids to take another man into their lives," she said. She got up then to check on the boys again, and Charlie looked at the back of Ann Marie's still head. Why couldn't the woman who'd moved in next door have been a little younger, no kids, and just a bit more attractive? he thought, and then immediately felt guilty. He could hear himself breaking the news at work if she had been that other woman: *Yep, getting married. And she literally was the girl next door.* He'd pass her picture around, and Rick would look at it in a way that showed he wished he'd met her instead, Stu trying to imagine her naked.

Melanie came back to the table, eyebrows raised, waiting for his answer. "No, I'm not dating anyone these days," he said.

She smiled, and right then she did look reasonably attractive—she had a nice face, really. *Needs to do something with herself*—that's what Lola would say. He shivered; his mother's voice in his head signaled impending psychosis, to be sure. Melanie patted his arm. "I thought so. I mean, no offense, but I read people pretty well. Comes in handy."

"For what? All your web sites?" Charlie said, and it came out more harshly than he'd intended. "Sorry," he said, shaking his head, looking at the floor. He felt miserable. He was the boy his father had slapped. He was sullen, full of himself.

"Hey, it's fine," Melanie said. "I didn't mean to offend you. Anyway, I might as well tell you, since I can tell you're an understanding person."

"It's okay," Charlie said. He had a strong desire not to know whatever she thought he'd be understanding about.

"I fulfill tele-fantasies."

Charlie looked at her. Melanie looked back at him, eyebrows raised, as if he had missed a fairly simple punch line. But she was serious. "I do phone sex?" she said. She barely dropped her voice.

Charlie looked over at Ann Marie; the girl hadn't moved, transfixed now with Scooby Doo. Charlie remembered having had a thing for Daphne. The whole situation there at the breakfast bar had gotten very confusing. Charlie thought of the big black file cabinet and looked back toward the office. The door was closed.

"And that is really where I work," she said. "Want to see?"

"No," Charlie said, standing up.

"Aw come on," she said, laughing, standing up, too. "Admit it. You've probably always wondered what the inside story is on that kind of thing."

Charlie had not thought about it much, and he suspected he wasn't alone in this; it was how people charged five dollars a minute for heavy breathing or whatever. It was enough for him to watch the women on late-night cable beckoning with their bikinis and nine-hundred numbers. He had never called; he could get warmed up enough just from the thirty-second commercial and could handle it on his own from there.

Melanie was between him and the door. "Wait a minute," she said. She opened the door and leaned out and the boys' voices drifted up in echoes from the parking lot. The sky was heavy and dark, but Melanie seemed satisfied. "Okay," she said. "Come on."

Charlie followed her down the hall. "Ann Marie sleeps with me," she said, pointing into one bedroom. "And the boys have the other room." He felt as if he had tripped and was still falling. He imagined other people seeing him in this situation, following a phone sex worker into her bedroom-slash-office. His mother horrified, Rick and Stu laughing, his sister rooting for him. His face felt hot and he knew he was blushing.

Melanie opened the door and flipped on the light. "Come in," she said, seeing him hesitate. He stepped into the room. There was a lamp and a recliner chair covered with a pink comforter in one corner, the filing cabinet in the other corner, and the computer on a clean desk against the opposite wall. There was barely enough space for two people to stand without touching. Melanie leaned over the desk, and Charlie, standing inches away from her hip, could see her breasts sway forward as she bent. He realized he was holding his breath and tried to exhale quietly. "That's me with the kids and the Ex at Disney World last year," she said, pointing to the image floating in a small circle on the screen. Charlie could see Melanie smiling with her three kids standing in front of her, smaller versions of themselves, smiling squinty kid smiles at the camera. Behind them rose the spires of the Magic Kingdom, everything sun-saturated and brilliant. "It's my screen saver," she said. She pressed a keyboard button, and the image disappeared. A plain blue-green screen blinked on in its place. Then a gray box appeared and she typed in some numbers, which appeared as asterisks. "I keep everything locked," she said, watching the screen.

Charlie felt an urge to compliment her conscientiousness, because it seemed she'd thought it through, but he didn't want to overuse the compliment tactic in case he had to resort to it later. It seemed likely that he would. She typed some more, and an image popped up on the screen of a woman in a long black wig, squatting in red platform heels, upper arms squeezing her huge bare breasts together in a way that barely hid the nipples, one hand slipping into her bikini bottom. Across the top of the screen, it said "CALL FELICIA FOR ALL YOUR FANTASIES."

"That's me. What do you think?" Melanie said. She seemed to be trying to decide, too. She sipped her beer.

"Yikes," Charlie said.

"People love her."

"People?"

"I have a few female clients." She leaned to close the window on her sexpot doppelganger. "I have clients who will only work with me. I have like thirty different roles—damsel in distress, cheerleader, dominatrix, schoolteacher, French maid, the usual. But then I have this one guy who only wants me to sing nursery rhymes and another who wants me to yell at him like his ex-wife. I keep it all in there," she said, pointing to the file cabinet.

"Well," Charlie said, sticking hands in his pockets and then, worried how it might look, pulling them out again. "That's great."

"I know, it's a lot to drop on you," Melanie said, as her screen saver popped back up. She ushered him out of the room and closed the door behind them. "But the kids are staying with their aunt this weekend, so I need to work in a little extra cash."

They walked back to the kitchen. She seemed to be trying to explain herself, but Charlie didn't get it. She read his expression and shook her head. "You poor thing," she said. "What I'm trying to say is, these walls here are paper-thin. I can hear you talking in the shower. You were going to find out anyway."

Charlie leaned against the breakfast bar at this revelation. Generally his shower monologues were directed to Stu for his overall callousness and reticence on pay raises, or to his mother, suggesting therapy, or, occasionally to his father, demanding explanations. Often he grew quite passionate, emerging from the shower red-faced, not just from the steam, but his own sentiments. He felt lightheaded, disoriented. He remembered coming into this kitchen every week to collect Ruby's trash when he was taking his own to the dumpster. He filled huge bags, having never hopped on the recycling bandwagon, but her little white plastic grocery bags contained only blue tissues, it seemed; he'd always wondered about it. Yet he'd been comfortable with that mystery and wished, currently, for a little more of it.

"It's no big deal," Melanie continued. "We all have our ways."

At first Charlie had thought she was talking about her services, how they were perfectly acceptable, and he certainly agreed, but then he suspected she'd been talking about his shower habits. He merely nodded, looking out the window, marveling at how quickly he'd shifted from a young, helpful neighbor to a frustrated shower-talker. Then, outside, sunlight glinted briefly on the stair railings, and the rain came in a silvery sheet over the roofs of the apartments across the quad, fat drops slapping the concrete breezeway. He thought he could even feel some spray coming through the screened upper half of the storm door. Melanie swung it open. "Boys!" she yelled. "Get in here now!"

Charlie followed her. "I should go, too."

"You don't have to," Melanie said. Charlie saw it then. He knew he wasn't good with women, couldn't read them at all except to judge whatever quality it was that made them right for his photographs. But he could tell she liked him; he saw it in the disappointed way she smiled. "But I understand. Tomorrow's another long day, right?"

"Thanks for dinner," Charlie said. He got out just as the boys thundered up the stairs and ran shouting past him as if they had not seen him at all.

HIS SISTER CALLED the next night. "Warning, warning!" she said. "I just got off the phone with Mom and she's heading your way."

"Crap," Charlie said, looking around at his apartment strung with cast-off clothes and unwashed dishes. "I better go clean."

"Wait. Mom was wanting the dirt on your love life. I told her I thought you were dating someone so if she calls you on it, play along."

"Okay." Charlie pinched the phone to his cheek with his shoulder and started picking up laundry.

"So are you?"

"Well, I had dinner with a woman yesterday. How's that?" He imagined his sister biting her hangnails, a habit since childhood, probably still at work, calling on the company dime. She loved him and worried for him; he knew this. He felt she was the only person in his life who actually wanted him to be happy as opposed to someone else entirely.

"Very good. Is she *the one?*" she asked, jokingly emphasizing the last two words. It was the kind of thing their mother asked.

"I doubt it," he said, stacking dishes in the sink and hunting a paper towel to wipe down the counter.

"Well, what's her deal? What's she do?"

Charlie opted for Melanie's official version of things. "She's a

Web site designer." He found a napkin from a pizza delivery and wet it down in the sink.

"Oh really? What's she done? I'll check them out."

"I don't know. You know I don't know anything about that stuff."

"Just ask her, dummy. Women like it when you ask them about their lives."

"Thanks for the advice." He could see his mother pulling up next to his car. "And for the warning. She's here."

"And another thing. Dad's in town."

Charlie could hear his sister breathing, waiting on the line. Partly she wanted to shock him, but she was looking out for him, too, trying to soften the blow of what his mother was certainly coming to tell him. "I gotta go," was all he could manage. He hung up, stuffed some dirty towels under the couch and shut his bedroom door.

He locked the front door, sat down and turned the television on low, listening to the click of his mother's heels up the concrete steps. She tried the door before knocking. He stayed where he was, heart pounding, thinking about his father. He'd seen him a couple of times in the first years, after he'd moved out, but then there had been no more visits or news.

"Honey?" his mother called, knocking, not a couple of knocks but a continuous peppering.

He opened up. His mother looked stricken. Even fully made up, with her dyed-black hair tucked smartly behind her ears and teased on top, she looked disheveled. She stepped into him—he didn't have time to get out of the way—and began crying. He put his arms around her, certain she would be able to feel how he was shaking. "Mom?"

"He's here for some trade show. Your father. That bastard had the nerve to call me." She sniffled against his T-shirt and he led her inside, where she collapsed on the couch. "You have anything to drink around here?"

"Beer or Pepsi," Charlie said. His mother wrinkled her nose. The only thing he'd ever seen her drink was white zinfandel, and not very often.

"Put it in a glass, please," she said, not specifying the beer but meaning that, Charlie knew. She hunted in her purse for a tissue, and, not finding one, stood to head for the bathroom, but Charlie got ahead of her. "Let me get it for you," he said. "Just sit down and try to relax."

Surprisingly, his mother obeyed. In his wrecked bathroom, he lowered the toilet seat quietly, pulled the shower curtain closed and ripped off several squares of toilet paper. He folded them as neatly as he could, then brought them to her with an opened beer and a glass. She blew her nose, poured the beer, tried one sip, grimaced and set it on the coffee table. It was a mark of how upset she was that she didn't admonish him for not having any real tissues. She took a deep breath and shook her head as Charlie sat beside her with his own beer, which was still in the can.

"You're going to have to go see him," she said.

"Why?" Charlie said. He did want to see him, but only because he wanted things he was pretty sure he couldn't have, like an explanation, or requests for a new start. Things didn't work out like that, he knew. The only perfect moments were the ones people snapped pictures of, to preserve them, of course, but also to have something to string together at the end, to tell themselves or others that this was the way life was, full of vacations and smiling kids playing in the backyard or holding up red M&Ms, a life coated with the promise of sweetness just ahead.

"Because he asked us to go. Your sister too, but naturally the jerk didn't even know she lives so far away."

Oddly, Charles bristled at his father being called a jerk. "Did you say you wouldn't go?"

His mother sniffed, shook her head. "I said I'd let you know. So you can go. Go meet him for dinner, play golf, whatever he does these days."

It wouldn't have helped to ask why he had to be the one to settle up, to show the sum of himself after all these years; how he'd chosen not to take advantage of all of his early privileges—education, smarts, a good profile—letting them melt away when others had not, or were born with none of these advantages, none at all.

"He's staying at the Seaside," his mother said, and then she closed her eyes and drained the rest of her beer.

And so the next night he found himself standing near the crowded bar of the Seaside Lounge, looking for his father. On the phone, his father had insisted that Charlie would recognize him, but Charlie had still asked what color shirt he'd be wearing. *Teal,* his father had barked. He winced, thinking of his father's impatience on the phone, the clipped, gravelly voice so like what he remembered, harsh like the face that had glared down at him after the slap, dismissing him and then disappearing. He dressed carefully, in khakis and a black long-sleeved button-down shirt because he felt it hid his gut. Right before walking out, he decided to bring his camera. This way he could tell himself it was a job. He was a freelance photographer and his job right now was to document a bumpy episode in his life. He took it out of his sculptured bag and put it in a satchel that said Siesta Key so it wouldn't be so obvious.

The bar was jammed with honeymooners and business travelers and packs of middle-aged men on golfing packages. The retirees had long since gone home after the early bird specials. His father would be one of those guys, sunburned from the links, eyeballing the waitresses. He looked for the teal shirt. When he saw him, there was no doubt: he looked like a slightly more squared-off version of Charlie. His coloring was darker and his hair was salt-and-pepper gray, though still thick. His skin looked thicker, too, maybe from the sun. He was sitting alone in a two-person booth. Charlie positioned himself behind the hostess' podium and tried to focus his Pentax, but his hands were shaking. Anybody passing by would have thought he was taking pictures of fellow vacationers.

And that could have been true; that could have been his life, lived anywhere else in the country or even the world, coming here just to blow some cash and try to hook up. The hostess ignored him as he fumbled and clicked off a couple shots of his father hunched over a menu, sipping a beer, a pack of cigarettes next to his right hand. He hadn't remembered his father smoking. His mother had never mentioned it.

Charlie was thinking this and aiming for one last shot when his father looked up and locked onto him, as if he'd known he'd been there the whole time. His father stood up, tossed his napkin on the table. Charlie stuffed the camera into his satchel, but it was too late. He focused on not stumbling as he wove his way through the loud patrons and stood at the end of the table, unable to think of what to say or do.

"You a spy?" his father demanded. His hair was a silvery helmet, every wire in place. He stuck his hands in his pockets and jingled his change.

Charlie looked down at his satchel. "I do photography on the side."

"On the side for who?"

Charlie shrugged, looked away. He wondered if years ago when his father had rendered him speechless, if that had been when he'd decided he was a graceless child, worth leaving. "Mom couldn't come," he said.

"So she sent you, hmm?"

Charlie wished he had the guts to be this direct with his father. He would have preferred it if the old man had shown up at Camera Town. He would have handed him film and Charlie would have known what to do with it. Days later, he'd have returned to pick up the proofs. And Charlie could have told him why certain shots hadn't turned out. But in this situation he felt muddled. There was nothing he could explain. "Yeah, that's pretty much it," he said.

"Have a seat," his father grunted, as he dropped heavily back onto the cushion. Charlie put his satchel on the seat and slid in next to it.

"Beer?"

Charlie nodded and his father raised one finger to the waitress, pointed to his beer, then pointed to Charlie. He turned back to Charlie, confident his need would be taken care of. "So really, what's with the pictures?" He laughed. "Is that what you do? Sneak around and play Candid Camera?"

"Pretty much," Charlie said. He rolled the edge of the paper menu. There were ones like it all over town, advertising oysters by the dozen and half, steamed, raw, broiled, fried. *How do you like it?* the cartoon mermaid on the menu asked. "I didn't know you smoked."

"Yeah, you probably don't remember too much about me, do you?" His father reached for the pack then, shook one out. Watching him light up, Charlie thought that was probably how he lived with having left—thinking no one remembered much. Or maybe he didn't need to believe anything in order to live with it.

"The truth is, Mom didn't really want to come," Charlie said, trying to make his tone match his attempt at bluntness. But his voice sounded thin, whiney.

"Didn't think she would." His father took a long drag on the cigarette, followed by a gulp of beer. "Probably didn't like the news I was getting married again."

The waitress brought the beers, and Charlie was grateful for the distraction. His mother had failed to mention this, too. "Congratulations," he said, and his father flashed a narrow-eyed smile, reading Charlie's surprise.

"She's a real estate broker." He pulled out his wallet, flipped it open, and Charlie saw a forty-something blonde woman in a white suit, heels and a lot of makeup, leaning against a tree, the way women often did when dressed up like that. "I'm not shocked your mother didn't tell you, frankly," his father said. "I mean, after I left her for someone else in the first place." He took another drag, coughed, and looked past Charlie's shoulder at the crowded room, where presumably he would see something of greater interest than his estranged son.

Charlie tried to disguise the fact that he had not known any of this. He looked down at the menu. He read *Grilled shrimp shish kabob with tangerine-infused soy sauce* three times silently and then gazed back at his father as calmly as he could manage. "She was probably just trying to protect us," Charlie said.

"Herself, more likely, to get the jump on any reality that might stray in her direction," his father said. "First she insisted that you and your sister not meet Donna, so after a while I stopped visiting. Then Donna left me," he threw his hands out as if to say easy come, easy go. "But by then, so much time had passed. I couldn't really see what meddling with you kids again would do." His father stubbed out his cigarette. "Anyway, me and Loreen are getting hitched, and you're invited if you want to come. Next month in Phoenix." He smiled, and Charlie smiled too, the way he did when Stu made jokes about his nudies in the developer room. He couldn't help himself; he just played along. He was that kind of guy. He drank his beer in long gulps.

"So how's your sister?" his father asked, not waiting for Charlie's response to his invitation. It had not in fact been a real invitation; Charlie understood this. The idea took form for him as clearly as a darkroom image floating up from its chemical bath. His father hadn't made a special trip to deliver his nuptial news, but it had been important to him to do so once a business trip had presented an opportunity. He was marrying a blonde, for God's sake. He had news any man could appreciate.

"Rose is fine, living in Cleveland," Charlie said. It was snowing up there; he'd seen on the news. He pictured his sister alone in her office, which he had never seen, but he could imagine it, a gray room wrapped with gray sky. He wondered what she would say to the wedding invitation. She was the older one; she remembered more than he did.

"Not married yet, I gather." He lit another cigarette.

"Nope."

"And you neither! Well, I guess I've been married enough times for all of us. Or almost," his father said, and it was an attempt at a joke, or his version of one. He laughed and ordered another beer. "You?" he asked Charlie.

"No thanks." He watched his father drain his drink. "You know, I do have one memory of you, real clear," Charlie said. "You slapped me once. Not long before you left. You remember that?" He said it half-smiling, as if they were recalling a holiday gathering where a lot of things gone wrong—the turkey afire, the garage flooded—but everyone had pulled through. Except, in this case, they had scattered, and knew almost nothing of each other.

His father seemed to be making an effort to recall. He shook his head. "Well, it's been a long time."

"It's what I think of when I think of you," Charlie said. He smiled the way he would when thanking a customer. "Clear as a picture." He grabbed his satchel and worked his way out of the booth as gracefully as he could. "I'll tell everyone you said hi," he said, as much to the noisy restaurant as to his father. He thought of how it had been for his father, packing a bag, jogging down the front steps of the house where his mother still lived—he'd always jogged down those steps, Charlie remembered—walking into his new life. He walked away, not waiting for an answer.

When he got home, he thought of knocking on Melanie's door, but it was late and her lights were off. Her kids' swimsuits hung in a row over the breezeway railing. There were, as he expected, several messages from his mother and one from his sister, all asking what had happened. He didn't know what he would be able to say to satisfy them. He undressed and stretched out in bed, unable to sleep. Then he heard moaning coming from Melanie's apartment. He sat up, listening. It came from the other side of his bedroom wall, which would be her office. It was a sexual moan, and it was her silky voice, he knew. He got up and walked closer to the wall.

He put his hand where he thought her recliner with the pink comforter might be. Then he heard her talking. She was pleading, actually, and when he pressed his ear to the wall he could understand the words. "Don't tickle me with that!" she was saying. Her voice was like something swirled and jiggling in a china bowl. "You want to spank me again, do you?" A playful squeal, then moaning.

Charlie wasn't sure what to do—turn on the TV and thump around so she'd know he was there? Meanwhile, he could feel a heat spreading in his thighs, tightening in the crotch. Here was an improvement on old Ruby's deaf ravings, but he knew he wasn't going to get any sleep. He got up, pulled on his jeans, zipped them with some difficulty, opened a beer and clicked on the television. Even with that, he could hear her voice in the background, rising and falling. It seemed to be the same phone call, on and on. How long could a guy go? he wondered, unzipping his jeans again and stroking himself idly as Jay Leno told jokes to what sounded like an extremely aroused and giggly audience. He heard smacking sounds then and felt too ridiculous to masturbate. You had to get over that, the image of yourself hunched over, pants down, wrist flicking back and forth, face blank in concentration. Here, he thought, was humanity at its simplest, when we were closest to our primate cousins. This idea had presented itself to him at the circus one night as a pinstripe-suited gorilla proceeded to get himself off in a totally improvised part of a comedy tap dance scene in the center ring. It had been impressively quick, the gorillas herded off mid-routine, and the show had gone on. Afterward, he met the woman who mistook him for the piano player, and at his apartment she'd broken into fresh laughter every time she'd looked at him. He didn't know why—because he wasn't the piano player? The possible reasons seemed endless. He'd been so eager for sex, he'd let her climb on him anyway. He'd easily matched the gorilla's time.

Jay Leno swiveled back and forth, dutifully delivering his closing punch line. His neck and shoulders appeared to be fused. Charlie thought that life was really made for the gorillas among us. People like his father, who could do what was expected of them most of the time—get married, go on business trips—but could also do whatever else he wanted without shame.

Things were quiet next door. Charlie turned down the TV and heard Melanie padding around in her apartment, the refrigerator door opening and closing. Ruby had always gone to bed by eight, and he'd never had to pay attention to the noise he made. He could hear every move Melanie made, especially now that it was night and the road traffic had quieted to an occasional whisper. Then he heard her front door open and close. He stood up and peeked out his door.

Melanie turned at the sound. She wore sweatpants and a long T-shirt that fit snugly at her hips. She was sipping from the narrow orange straw of a juice box, the kind of thing she probably packed in her kids' lunches. In the crook of her other arm hung the kids' swimsuits, which she'd collected from the railing. She raised her juice box to him in a joking toast. "And what have you been up to tonight?" she asked. She smiled, but she looked tired under the dim yellow overhead lights, shadows lining the slight drape of skin under her jaw.

"Oh, seeing my father for the first time in, let's see, about twenty-four years now," Charlie said, relieved to say exactly what came to mind.

"Oh, my," Melanie said, concern drawing her eyebrows together.

"Well, that's not right," Charlie said. It seemed important to get it right. "I did see him a couple of times after he left, so I guess we could call it an even twenty."

"Charlie," she said, walking to him, reaching for his hand. He let her take it, and she led him inside her apartment. He sat down on the couch and felt something crunch under him, a potato chip.

"Did you hear the racket?" she said as she sat down beside him. "The guy wanted a marathon. It's all props, I'm telling you. I don't have any real sex toys, per se, though just about anything can be a sex toy depending on who you're dealing with, believe me. Sometimes I steal one of the kid's lollipops or fruit bars if I need—"

"Please," Charlie said. He leaned his head back against the cushion. "I don't want to know how you do all that. Really." He felt tired enough to close his eyes and sleep right there.

"Yeah, I wouldn't want to ruin the romance for you," she said, but when he looked over at her, she was smiling. She patted his hand. "So what'd your father want?"

"I don't know. To show off his great life, I guess," Charlie said. "He started off with my mom and me and my sister, and then he left for someone else and now he's marrying some woman in Phoenix."

Melanie set her empty juice box on the TV stand. The room was so small she only had to lean forward from her perch on the couch to reach it. "Some men are just five-minute types of guys," she said. "You know, they think about five minutes ahead, and they want things in five minutes, because that's where the bargain is. The first five minutes are cheap."

Melanie's voice sounded like poured honey, but she was biting her lip, looking at her lap, as if regretting what she'd just said. Charlie figured if Melanie had five minutes on the phone with his father, she'd know all there was to him. He considered suggesting this, then decided against it. He thought of the women on the phone sex commercials, and the people he took pictures of, and why he chose them. Taking pictures was the right way to say it. You took the picture because you wanted something from it: To preserve things that leave you, like beauty, or affection, or the truth of a situation. His prints were stacked in photo paper boxes under his bed. His favorite image currently was of an old man pressing his nose to a tomato, eyes closed, the fruit cradled in his palm. He loved the smooth skin of the fruit against the mottled skin of the old man's hand. He loved how the man had closed his eyes, as if to better drink in the scent.

"I'd like to show you some photos," he said to Melanie. Then, so she wouldn't think he meant Stu's brand of photography, he said, "I mean, I'm a photographer."

"That would be great," she said.

He got up to get them but then, in the breezeway on the way to his door, he stood still to listen to the ocean. During the day you couldn't hear it over the traffic, but at night it was a breathing presence. He wasn't sure he wanted to tip his hand, call it all out in the open the way Melanie had. Because you could believe anything you wanted about your dreams or your abilities, and things still were what they were. He willed Melanie's phone to ring, something to make him change course. He heard nothing but the pulling ocean, the murmur of his TV. He turned to walk inside, to drag his pictures from the dark.

Plot vs. Character

H E'S THE ONLY GUY I ever met at a bar and then took to bed. He was twenty-nine and in town from Baltimore for the summer, overseeing the renovation of the old courthouse, living out of a Holiday Inn. I was twenty-one, a broadcast cinema major with an acceptance letter in my back pocket from a film school in England for a year of study. I was celebrating. He bought me a drink and asked if I knew the bar we were in was once the town's cathouse. He was tall and lean and green-eyed, but not pretty—nose had maybe been broken, chipped front tooth, some nice wear and tear. Smiling, yet very serious about his history lesson. He stamped the floor. "Solid," he said.

Kissing him on what occurred to me was a rather rickety footbridge over the river, I realized I was with what appeared to be a grown man. Compared to the beer slugging, monosyllabic fratheads comprising the college selection, he was good with words, good with his hands. I decided to trust him not to kill me, and took him to my place.

For the rest of the summer, we went to bad movies, then to the river's edge and had sex so hard our bodies turned nearly 360 degrees on the blanket. Sometimes I went to his motel room, but he liked it best outside, and I found I did too. "I enjoy a little dirt in my hair," he said, and I obliged, pressing his shoulders into the damp ground.

At summer's end there was no breakup, just the two of us

wrapped in a polyester bedspread on the concrete slab balcony outside his room, his breath still coming hard, hands on my hips, as he told me he couldn't believe I was leaving. Of course, he was leaving, too. But this was part of his appeal, how he could appear to be heartbroken when this was not in fact the case. And I fell for it—for him. I'll just admit that now.

I went to England, distracted myself with red-cheeked British boys, came home, graduated, and took a job with a small video production company where I edited low-budget corporate presentations, commercials, product demos and the occasional soap opera episode. He became the story I told my friends. I said, trying to sound nonchalant, "The best thing about it was we knew how it would end."

But of course I should've known better, right? How does knowing the end help anything? There are women who would've moved on from this as neatly as a housewife trades out her old detergent when a new brand comes along. I've met them, but I could never be one of them, no matter how much I tried to convince myself. Here's the truth about me: I was a clingy sort, hoarding old toothbrushes and my stuttering TV, things that begged retirement. I tried the usual strategies—working a lot, rearranging my apartment furniture—but inevitably my mind rolled to the builder like a marble on a slanted floor. The feeling emerged like hunger, or being too cold, and usually at the end of the evening, after I'd gone from work to gym to errands to the freezer for another pre-packaged dinner.

Eventually, a fantasy took shape. It went like this: A location shoot takes me to Baltimore, where the builder lives, still single. We have dinner. He invites me back for a long weekend (but now, looking back, I wonder why did I have to come to him, even in the fantasy?) There are sizzling nature walks in the Shenandoah Valley. We get married.

Here's what really happened. A year passed. I got back from a location shoot in Atlanta and there was a voicemail from Baltimore.

The builder was in Winston-Salem for the weekend, pitching new business. He took me to dinner at a restaurant in an historic inn, and we sat in the candlelit garden room with floor-to-ceiling open windows. He was still lean and well-muscled, and yet he also looked older, tired around the eyes, which for some reason made me want to exhaust him further. He looked at me as if he might pull me with him to the floor at any moment; instead he tipped back his chair and stroked the wainscoting with a fingertip. The message was clear: *this fingertip wants to trace your lines, too, honey.*

How *done* this was, really, the long gaze, then the eyes averted as if he was frightened by his desire. If you outlined the average soap episode, which I unfortunately did often, for pay, you'd see at least three of these loaded stares, and not more than five, in forty-four minutes. And yet I must admit how well it worked on me. After we ate, he insisted on walking to my car, to protect me, of course, from the many roaming men the city teemed with who would want to kidnap me on sight. I knew very well how much danger I was in, but when he took me in his arms I froze like a netted rodent, heart flicking in my throat, wondering what he would do. But the builder was interested in an innocent full-body hug, of which he determined the closeness and the duration. I walked away, still clinging to certain notions about the smart, carefree woman I wanted to believe I was. It was a conflicting persona, though. The carefree woman would sleep with a man because she wanted to; the smart woman knew her limits, and this man exceeded them.

Why? Here's what I knew about the builder, which is to say, what I'd started to suspect about myself: I was in love not so much with him, but the idea of him, which strongly featured the dual characteristics of handiness and a love for modern literature (well, he'd hinted at reading Hemingway and had once asked me if he should dare to eat a peach, but I think he'd been talking about something other than the paralysis of desire). He was an image to me, not exactly a man. I knew this, but knowing didn't make me want him any less.

Nevertheless, when he called the next day I showed up, and—surprise—he led me up a shady trail above the Blue Ridge Parkway. It was sunny but humid from recent rain; I watched him wind through rhododendron and I got all confused, turned on by the smell of wet earth. Then dinner again; I was so hungry I was sweating and my legs were wobbly from all those slippery inclines. I was exhausted, but when he suggested a movie I heard myself saying yes. What was the movie even about? I don't know—there was a green dress, a blown-up car, subtitles. But I did know the storyline from there: the arm sliding around my shoulders, the voice dropping to a whisper, all that nutritious blood my brain needed draining straight to my crotch.

Back at his hotel room, I realized I had no idea if he had a home, or if that leather bag on the luggage stand, the same one from two years ago, was all there was. He laid me on the bed fully clothed, took his shirt off. I could feel how hard he was as he pressed down on me again.

The phone rang so loud we both jerked away from each other, startled. He sat up, answered it, listened for a moment.

"Maribel," he said. I sat up, cheeks hot, nipples hard, underwear soaked. *Maribel?* Who the fuck was that? Who had a name like that anymore? Oh, I could see her—she was small-boned and dark-haired; she blushed easily and owned pottery. I wanted him to say he'd call her back—because it was too much to ask the gods for him to say *I thought you understood, it's over; I've found who I want*—and right then I realized that for all my fantasizing, I'd really been waiting for this one scene. I needed dramatic tension, and there we were.

He was hunched forward, elbows on his knees, one palm propping his forehead, the other clutching the phone. Not even an apologetic glance my way. *Get up get up!* I screamed at myself, but I was still sitting there, straining to hear her voice, trying to figure out what she was saying that had such power over him.

"You fucked me," he said then. "You fucked me over." Not an

accusation, a complaint begging consolation. I managed to swing my legs over the edge of the bed, my toes digging into the worn carpet, searching for balance. "Wait," he said, turning to me when he felt the bed shift as I pushed myself to my feet. He reached for me, missed.

I slid on my shoes. "Look," he said, "I'll call you back." He hung up. So I got my wish, right? He said he'd call her back! Let me tell you, *that* felt like a victory.

"Is that your wife?" I managed to ask. I knew to keep going for the door; he'd follow. It was in every script: Chick runs stage right crying [*holds damp hankie*]; guy runs after her [*wears lipstick-stained shirt and rumpled pants*]. I had entered one of my own productions.

"Please come here," he said.

I knew this one. I was cued for my line: "Don't. I don't want to hear it."

"Just sit with me for a few minutes. I know you're going to go."

Tugging on my hand, he led me back to the bed. I allowed this to be enough persuasion to sit. I wasn't even sure I could drive. I was too exhausted, drunk, turned on. And another part of me, distant as a moon, orbited the planet that was myself, curious. What would he say? What would I do?

"I'm sorry," he said. Sticking with the script so far. He turned to me. Was he going to kiss me? I was about to laugh. But no, he hugged me, and this was worse. It was the break-up scene I thought I'd avoided. This ruined him as a good story, the one that made me look sexy, confident, free. It erased a future plotline I thought might be available to me. From then on, he could only be a flashback.

He slid his hands up the back of my shirt, talking into my hair, which I love. When he said he'd always felt he had to treat me with kid gloves because I was so young, I couldn't even raise an eyebrow and tell him to go back to his makeup trailer. *Up, up, up!* I could hear my muscles shrilling, but I let him hold me until he was ready to let go, and as I walked to the door, I knew there wouldn't be any speeches to stop me.

An unexpected scene a month later: Hallway of the low-ceilinged office building where I work. Guy in suit stands in front of the open double doors of the suite next to mine—heavy black-chrome eighties décor within—talking on a cell phone. I realize there's a pattern: guy in hallway, me passing, small talk, repeat. That morning he gives me his card, then asks me out. This is a new one.

The following Friday evening: A Japanese restaurant, warm and rainy outside; candlelit table, funny waiter is generous with sake. Guy looks better out of the suit. Brown hair, wide-set brown eyes, not too tall but taller than me. He tells me he's an engineer. I ask him if they still give out those striped caps. He laughs. He takes me home, the two of us sit on my bare wood floor and listen to music. I keep my distance because now I don't trust myself; the carefree/smart woman bit it that night in a hotel in Winston-Salem. She'd died young, barely formed, and now I'm an alcoholic at a martini bar when it comes to men; I have no judgment. This is what I've come to believe. When he leaves we're both playing it so cool we nearly shake hands.

The next morning, the phone wakes me but I miss the call. I dial voicemail, and who could it be but the builder with the cinematic sense of timing, taking my breath away with his casual hello? I call him back that evening, eager to keep a wounded but still vigorous fantasy alive. Of course, this all against my better judgment. Somewhere in my mind there resides a delicate connection with reality that knows I won't be satisfied. But the body remembers its desires long after they make any sense. You recite the old motions. Just like riding a bike.

So first, I prepare: a few glasses of wine, some jazz. By the time I call him, I think I *am* Billie Holiday. The builder tells me it's over between him and Maribel the potter. I don't miss a beat; I ask when he'll be in town next. He's not sure.

Then it comes to me, seeping somehow through the snowy

static of alcohol and hopefulness I've wrapped myself in. A moment of clarity: I know there's nothing I can say. Eventually I'll forgive myself my desires. So I tell him to let me know when he is sure, and hang up. I don't know if I'll hear from him again, but I do know this: the builder is interested in my admiration only so much as it feeds his ego. I can tell he's lonely, maybe a little desperate to know what his future holds—will he get married? Have children? Perhaps he wants these things, but not with me, that much is clear.

A week later. Sharing a six-pack with the engineer on the grass next to the retention pond behind his apartment building, watching the moon rise, just shy of full. This town is prickly with new complexes with names like Duck Run and Fox Hollow. He has no furniture. I ask about it. He asks me where mine is. I say, "I like the minimalist look." I don't tell him I never bought much because without realizing it I had been preparing for a move that wasn't going to happen. He nods. He's scared to kiss me; I know this. It used to turn me off, shyness in men, but now I like it. I decide I can wait for him to work up his courage.

Of course, there's one more message. The builder says he wants to "continue our previous conversation," which probably means he'll tell me he's not sure he wants me, but he'll say it in a way that will allow me to translate it into possible affection. My salvation is that I won't settle for it.

And what will not settling mean? This is fresh territory, a room so new I can smell the cut wood and drying plaster. I test the floor, open a window. Throw the script out, one page at a time.

QUINN DALTON is the author of a novel, *High Strung*, and a story collection, *Bulletproof Girl*. Stories have appeared in dozens of literary magazines and in anthologies such as *New Stories from the South: The Year's Best*. Visit www.quinndalton.com.

Cover Artist

MYLA KENT'S photography explores the people, beauty and rhythm of life in the Pacific Northwest. Her work has been featured on National Geographic.com, in *Seattle Magazine*, *JPG Magazine*, and in *File Magazine*. She can be found most days photographing urban life in and around downtown Seattle. Her work can be found at www.mylakent.com.